WHISPERS IN THE RADCLIFFE CAMERA

WHISPERS IN THE RADCLIFFE CAMERA

GAY CHRONICLES FROM OXFORD

GRIFF HOLLAND

Paperback ISBN: 9798871514696

Cover Design by Etienne St. Aubert

Book Design by Luca Holland

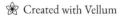 Created with Vellum

CONTENTS

1
OXFORD'S CHARM

Golden Dawn: A Moment Suspended in Time

Daniel Wilkinson wandered the cobblestone streets of Oxford as the first rays of dawn bathed the ancient buildings in gold. The air was crisp, carrying the scent of damp earth and blooming flowers, filling his lungs with freshness as he moved through the tranquil college town. His footsteps echoed softly against the stones as he admired the gothic spires piercing the sky, their intricate carvings and stained-glass windows glowing faintly in the morning light. Every corner of the city whispered secrets of scholars and poets who had walked these paths before him, but today, Daniel's thoughts were occupied by something far more immediate.

AN UNEXPECTED ENCOUNTER: TENSION BUILDS

As he turned a corner, his eyes locked on a familiar figure in the distance. Leaning casually against an ivy-covered wall stood Alex Duquesne, his lean body framed by the early light. Daniel's pulse quickened as he picked up his pace.**"Good morning,"** Daniel called softly, startling Alex, who turned quickly, flashing a disarming smile.

"Daniel! You scared the hell out of me," Alex laughed, pushing away from the wall. **"What brings you out so early?"**

Daniel shrugged, trying to appear nonchalant despite the way his heart pounded. **"Couldn't resist the sunrise,"** he said with a grin. **"Oxford's never more beautiful than at this hour."**

They fell into step, walking side by side as the golden light played across their features. Daniel found himself stealing glances at Alex —his tousled hair, the sharp angle of his jawline, and the slight curve of his lips.

"This place is magic," Alex mused, his voice low and thoughtful. **"Sometimes I feel like I'm living in a dream. It's so perfect it almost doesn't seem real."**

Daniel nodded but couldn't tear his gaze away from Alex's face. **"You make it seem even more unreal,"** he blurted, the words escaping before he could stop them.

Alex turned, his eyes locking onto Daniel's, and for the briefest moment, time froze.

The Bench Beneath the Oak: A Confession Unfolds

They reached a secluded bench under a sprawling oak tree, its branches sheltering them from the world. As they sat, Daniel's pulse raced, his senses alive to the subtle heat radiating from Alex's body.

"Do you ever wish we could just freeze time?" Daniel asked softly. **"Stay right here, like this, forever?"**

Alex held his gaze, the faintest smile tugging at his lips. **"Some-times,"** he admitted. **"But I also think life's too short to waste wishing for stillness. It's meant to be felt."**

Their knees brushed, and Daniel felt a jolt of electricity. He swallowed hard, his gaze dropping to Alex's lips—full, inviting, and slightly parted.

Without thinking, Daniel reached out, his fingers brushing against Alex's hand. Alex didn't pull away. Instead, he turned his palm upward, letting their fingers intertwine.

"What if I said I didn't want to waste time?" Daniel whispered, leaning in closer.

Alex's breath hitched. **"Then I'd say stop wasting it."**

Daniel closed the distance, his lips capturing Alex's in a soft, tentative kiss. Alex responded instantly, deepening it, his tongue sliding against Daniel's as heat flared between them.

Passion Unleashed: Desire Takes Over

Hands roamed hungrily, exploring muscles and flesh through layers of clothing. Daniel slid his palm down Alex's chest, feeling the firmness beneath, before reaching his belt and tugging it open.

"You sure about this?" Alex whispered, his voice heavy with need.

"I've never been more sure about anything," Daniel replied, his lips grazing Alex's neck.

Alex groaned as Daniel's hands slipped under his waistband, gripping his firm ass and pulling him closer. Their cocks strained against the fabric, grinding together and creating unbearable friction.

"Fuck," Alex panted. **"Touch me. Now."**

Daniel obliged, freeing Alex's cock and wrapping his fingers around it. He stroked slowly, savoring the way Alex's breath hitched and his hips bucked.

Heat of the Moment: Surrender

Alex pushed Daniel back onto the bench and straddled him, pulling his own shirt off and tossing it aside. Daniel followed suit, their bare chests pressing together as Alex began grinding his hips, their erections rubbing with delicious pressure.

"I want you so bad," Alex whispered, biting Daniel's ear.

"Take it," Daniel growled. **"I'm yours."**

Alex reached down, pulling lube from his bag—he'd clearly come prepared. He slicked Daniel's cock, guiding it to his entrance as he sank down slowly, the stretch making him moan loudly.

"Fuck, Daniel," Alex gasped, riding him with growing intensity.

Daniel gripped Alex's hips, thrusting up to meet him, their bodies moving in sync. The park, the world, and the rising sun all faded as they lost themselves in each other.

Climax and Afterglow: Bound Forever

Alex's moans grew louder, his cock bouncing against his stomach as Daniel pounded into him harder, deeper.

"I'm gonna cum," Alex groaned, stroking himself furiously.

"Do it," Daniel demanded, his thrusts growing erratic.

With a cry, Alex erupted, his cum spilling across Daniel's abs. The sight sent Daniel over the edge, and he buried himself deep, filling Alex with his hot load.

They collapsed together on the bench, panting and trembling as the aftershocks rippled through their bodies.

"**Holy shit,**" Alex muttered, still breathless. "**That was...**"

"**Incredible,**" Daniel finished, pulling him into a tight embrace. "**I'm not letting you go.**"

"**Good,**" Alex said, kissing him softly. "**Because I don't want you to.**"

As the sun climbed higher, bathing them in its warm glow, Daniel and Alex held each other, knowing this was only the beginning of something extraordinary.

A Spark Ignites

Daniel's heart hammered at Alex's words, recognizing the raw passion that pulsed beneath each syllable. He knew their connection could easily transcend mere acquaintance, that a deeper, more physical exploration was necessary for them to understand each other honestly. And so, without hesitation, Daniel abandoned caution, pulling Alex close and capturing his lips in an intense kiss that left them both breathless and trembling with anticipation. As they kissed beneath the warm, rising sun, Daniel knew that their journey was beginning—a path paved with passion, pleasure, and unforgettable experiences that would forever alter their lives.

"**Nice, dude,**" Alex whispered, pulling back.

"**I know, right? Are you open to exploring more?**" Daniel asked, a playful glint in his eyes.

Without hesitation, Alex replied, "Your place or mine. " His suggestive tone caused both young men to laugh.

Daniel suggested climbing the steps of the Radcliffe Camera. A sign to the side of the main entrance proclaimed the building open to visitors 24/7, but "unmonitored and unguarded."

"Interesting," Daniel said. "**This is my third year, and I've never been inside.**"

"**Me either. Let's give it a shot,**" Alex suggested, imagining the illicit possibilities of such a place.

The entrance was dimly lit and gloomy. Signs for restrooms and conference rooms lined the hall. The group moved towards a door marked "Quiet Study Room."

Daniel looked at the sign and raised an eyebrow. "**Quiet study room, huh? Sounds like a perfect place for some...private exploration,**" he said, his voice a husky whisper.

Alex grinned mischievously, his eyes sparkling with excitement. "**I couldn't agree more,**" he replied, his mind already picturing the thrilling encounters that could unfold in an unmonitored space.

INTO THE SHADOWS

They pushed open the heavy door, anticipation washing over them as they entered the dim room. The air was thick with the scent of old books and a faint, musky aroma of desire. Rows of bookshelves, packed with dusty tomes that whispered of forgotten secrets, lined the walls.

As they walked further in, Daniel's hand brushed against Alex's, their fingers intertwining in silent agreement. A soft glow from a desk lamp illuminated a secluded corner, calling them closer. They moved towards it, hearts pounding with the growing intensity of their desire.

Reaching the corner, Daniel pressed Alex against the wall, their bodies coming alive with a hunger that had been building for far too long. Their lips collided in a passionate kiss, their tongues tangling in a sensual dance. The taste of each other was intoxicating, driving their desire to explore every inch of one another.

Daniel's fingers worked deftly, undoing the buttons of Alex's shirt, revealing a toned chest that begged to be touched. He traced his fingertips along the defined muscles, relishing how Alex's breath hitched with each teasing caress.

Not to be outdone, Alex swiftly removed Daniel's shirt, exposing a sculpted physique that made his heart race even faster. He leaned in, his lips finding the sensitive skin of Daniel's neck, nipping and sucking with a hungry intensity that left a trail of fiery kisses.

Their hands roamed freely, exploring the contours of each other's bodies with an urgency that bordered on desperation. The room seemed to melt away, leaving only their shared desire and the intoxicating pleasure that consumed them.

As their bodies melded together, they found solace in the shadows, their moans of pleasure muffled by the peaceful atmosphere. The shelves of books stood witness to their passionate encounter, their spines trembling with the weight of the erotic energy that filled the room.

DESIRE UNLEASHED

Time dissolved as Daniel and Alex surrendered to the magnetic pull between them. Their bodies moved in perfect rhythm—hips grinding, breaths mingling—as if they were born to fit together. The dimly lit study room, once a shrine to knowledge, became a sanctuary for raw, unrestrained passion.

"God, I can't get enough of you," Daniel growled, his voice thick with hunger as he pressed Alex harder against the table.

"Then don't stop," Alex whispered, his lips parting in a gasp when Daniel's teeth grazed the sensitive skin of his neck.

GRIFF HOLLAND

Their hands roamed greedily, tugging at shirts and belts, desperate to feel bare skin. Each kiss, each touch, ignited a deeper craving, the heat between them intensifying until the air felt electric.

The scent of leather-bound volumes and aged parchment mixed with the musk of sweat and arousal. Their grinding bodies left damp stains on their trousers as cocks throbbed against the fabric, aching for release.

"You're so fucking hard," Alex hissed, his fingers slipping under Daniel's waistband to feel the slick heat pooling there.

Daniel grabbed Alex's wrist and guided him, gasping when fingers wrapped around his shaft, stroking slowly.

"Don't tease me," Daniel warned, his breath ragged.

"Then bend me over the table and take me."

The words hung in the air, dangerous and exhilarating. Daniel spun Alex around, bending him forward until his palms flattened against the dusty wood. Fingers tore at buttons and zippers, freeing their cocks, already dripping with anticipation.

Bound by Desire

Daniel's grip tightened on Alex's hips as he pushed his cock between the muscled curves of his ass, teasing the sensitive cleft.

"Beg for it," Daniel commanded, his voice low and dominant.

"Please," Alex panted, pushing back eagerly. **"I need you inside me."**

Spit slicked Daniel's cock before he pressed forward, the tight heat pulling a guttural moan from deep in his chest. He didn't ease in gently. He claimed Alex with deliberate, punishing thrusts, their moans echoing off the stone walls like forbidden hymns.

Books and papers shifted precariously, falling to the floor as the table rocked beneath them. Alex's hands gripped the edges, knuckles white as he surrendered to the delicious assault.

"Harder," he pleaded.

"Take it," Daniel growled, pounding relentlessly, sweat dripping down his back.

Daniel's grip tightened on Alex's hips as he pushed his cock between the muscled curves of his ass, teasing the sensitive cleft.

"Beg for it," Daniel commanded, his voice low and dominant.

"Please," Alex panted, pushing back eagerly. **"I need you inside me."**

Spit slicked Daniel's cock before he pressed forward, the tight heat pulling a guttural moan from deep in his chest. He didn't ease in gently. He claimed Alex with deliberate, punishing thrusts, their moans echoing off the stone walls like forbidden hymns.

Books and papers shifted precariously, falling to the floor as the table rocked beneath them. Alex's hands gripped the edges, knuckles white as he surrendered to the delicious assault.

"Harder," he pleaded.

"Take it," Daniel growled, pounding relentlessly, sweat dripping down his back.

A HIDDEN PARADISE

Slowly, they disentangled, their fingers brushing as they tucked themselves back into their clothes.

"I can't believe we just did that," Alex murmured, wiping sweat from his brow.

"Believe it," Daniel said with a smirk, brushing a kiss against Alex's swollen lips. **"And it won't be the last time."**

The study room, silent once more, bore witness to their illicit passion—its dusty air thick with the memory of desire. As they stepped out into the morning light, they exchanged numbers, knowing this was only the beginning of their journey into forbidden pleasure.

HAUNTED BY DESIRE

Night wrapped Oxford in its velvet embrace, but Daniel's bed felt anything but comforting. He lay there, restless, his skin still tingling with the memory of Alex's touch. The scent of leather and sweat lingered in his mind, mingling with echoes of Alex's husky whispers and the taste of his lips beneath the pale light of dawn at Radcliffe Camera.

He replayed every stolen moment—the heat of their grinding bodies, the hunger in their kisses—as his hand slipped beneath the waistband of his boxer briefs.

"What if we'd gone further?" he whispered into the empty room, his voice trembling with longing. **"What if I'd taken him right there on that table?"**

The thought gripped him, vivid and unrelenting. He imagined pressing Alex's body against the cool, dusty wood, their moans muffled by ancient tomes and stone walls.

His fingers teased the growing heat between his thighs, stroking slowly as his fantasies spiraled deeper. In his mind, Alex was on his knees, lips parted, eyes locked upward as he took Daniel's cock to the hilt.

"You taste so fucking good," Daniel murmured to no one, his hips bucking slightly as he imagined Alex's tongue working him over.

The fantasy shifted. Now Alex was bent over a desk, his trousers pooled at his ankles, begging for Daniel's cock.

"Please," Daniel moaned softly, losing himself in the vision of thrusting hard and deep, claiming Alex with every pounding stroke. **"Take it. Take every inch."**

His breath quickened. He gripped himself tighter, imagining Alex's moans echoing off the walls as Daniel filled him again and again, pushing him to the edge of surrender.

Pleasure and Possibility

The pressure built until Daniel couldn't hold back. His body arched as he spilled over his stomach, gasping Alex's name as pleasure rocked through him. For a moment, the fantasy felt real—too real—and the weight of desire lingered, leaving him flushed and aching for more.

"Thank you, universe," he whispered into the darkness, chest heaving as his fingers lazily traced the wetness on his skin.

The glow of his phone interrupted the silence. A text.

> Hope you had as much fun today as I did.
> Can't wait to see you again.

Daniel grinned, wiping himself clean before typing back.

> Me too. Can't stop thinking about it. We need
> to finish what we started.

Dreams of More

Sliding under the sheets, Daniel closed his eyes, but sleep didn't come easily. Images of Alex filled his dreams—naked, sprawled across bookshelves, restrained by silk ties, begging Daniel to take him harder.

"If only..." he muttered before drifting off, his mind already crafting new fantasies and new stories to tell—stories about forbidden encounters, untamed passions, and lovers who lost themselves in the depths of desire.

2
LATE-NIGHT PLEASURE

Forbidden Desires Unveiled

Night draped Oxford in shadows as Daniel slipped back into the Radcliffe Camera, his pulse quickening with curiosity and arousal. Under the dim flicker of ancient bulbs, the library felt transformed, its daytime solemnity replaced by an air of secrecy and seduction.

Daniel wandered through the aisles, trailing his fingertips along the spines of old books. But the study was the furthest thing from his mind. His thoughts were clouded by lust—memories of Alex, the heat of their encounter, and the hunger gnawing at him since.

That was when he saw it.

Rounding a corner, Daniel froze. A young man stood at one of the tables, his pants bunched around his ankles, stroking his cock in long, deliberate motions.

Daniel's breath caught. The sight was raw and obscene—a forbidden act playing out in this temple of intellect and history. But the stranger's confidence, the unashamed display of pleasure, sent a jolt of heat straight to Daniel's groin.

. . .

A Silent Invitation

For a moment, Daniel hesitated. But then the stranger's eyes met his, dark and inviting.

"Don't just stand there," the man said with a smirk, his voice low and teasing. **"Join me."**

Daniel's heart pounded as he stepped closer, his hands already undoing his belt.

"You sure about this?" Daniel murmured, his voice trembling as he freed his throbbing erection.

"Absolutely."

They stood facing each other, stroking themselves as their gazes locked—two strangers united by unspoken desire. The faint echoes of moans and footsteps hinted at others moving through the shadows, but Daniel didn't care. The air was thick with musk, and his pulse quickened with the thrill of exposure.

Unable to resist, Daniel dropped to his knees.

"Let me taste you," he said, his voice barely more than a whisper before he leaned in and wrapped his lips around the man's cock.

The stranger groaned, gripping Daniel's hair as he guided him deeper. Daniel took him eagerly, savoring the salty taste, the weight of it on his tongue. He worked his mouth with growing confidence, hollowing his cheeks and letting the man fuck his face.

"You're so fucking good at this," the stranger moaned, his hips bucking as he pushed deeper.

Daniel moaned around him, the vibration sending shudders up the man's spine. He loved the taste, the power of bringing another man to the edge. He wanted to own this moment, to leave this stranger trembling.

The Edge of Surrender

The stranger's breathing hitched, his grip tightening.

"I'm close," he gasped. **"Don't stop."**

Daniel sucked harder, taking him all the way until the man cried out, his cock pulsing as he spilled down Daniel's throat. Daniel swallowed greedily, the heat of it fueling his own desire.

As the man sagged against the table, Daniel stood, his own cock still aching for release.

"Turn around," he commanded, surprising himself with the sudden authority in his voice.

The man obeyed, bending over the table and presenting himself. Daniel spat into his hand, slicking himself quickly before pushing inside.

A Symphony of Lust

The library filled with the sounds of their bodies—skin slapping, heavy breathing, and the occasional gasp or moan that echoed through the stacks. Daniel drove into him hard and fast, the risk of discovery heightening every sensation.

"You like being used, don't you?" Daniel growled, his fingers digging into the man's hips.

"Yes! Fuck me harder!"

The words pushed Daniel over the edge. He thrust deep one last time, groaning as he came, spilling inside the stranger's trembling body.

They stood there afterward, panting, their bodies slick with sweat.

"That was..." the man started, but Daniel cut him off with a grin.

"Incredible. And I think we're just getting started."

Pulling up his pants, Daniel stepped away from the table and noticed movement in the shadows—figures watching, stroking themselves, waiting to join in.

He smirked.

"Looks like we're not the only ones who needed this tonight."

The Circle of Desire

Daniel's hunger hadn't faded—it had only grown. As more men stepped forward, shedding their clothes, Daniel knew this was no ordinary library. It was a sanctuary for lust, a place where bodies were books waiting to be opened and explored.

He dropped his pants again, ready to lose himself in the sea of bodies, cocks, and moans. Tonight, the Radcliffe Camera was alive—not with learning, but with sex.

And Daniel wasn't going to stop until he'd experienced everything it had to offer.

Daniel's body trembled, his hand working faster, pumping his cock as the chorus of moans and wet strokes filled the air around him. The scent of sweat, musk, and pre-cum saturated the historic room, turning the Radcliffe Camera into a sanctuary of forbidden pleasure.

Men grunted and gasped in unison, their bodies glistening in the dim light as they stroked themselves shamelessly. Daniel surrendered to the rhythm, his cock pulsing as he edged closer to climax.

"Fuck... I'm gonna cum," he hissed, his voice barely audible over the sounds of pleasure echoing through the stacks.

The moment hit him like lightning—a surge of heat and ecstasy that exploded through his body. Hot ropes of cum shot across his fingers, splattering onto the floor as he moaned, completely lost in the moment.

A HUNGER AWAKENED

Panting and flushed, Daniel leaned back against the table, his chest heaving as he surveyed the scene. Men wiped themselves clean, their eyes lingering on one another with silent invitations. He could feel it—the hunger still simmering beneath their skin.

"What the hell just happened?" he muttered, wiping the sweat from his brow.

But he already knew. This wasn't just lust—it was freedom, indulgence, and discovery, all tangled together in a single, primal act.

As he dressed and slipped out of the library, Daniel's thoughts raced. What other secrets lay hidden within these walls? What forbidden pleasures awaited him if he dared to return?

Meanwhile, Alex couldn't shake the restless energy coursing through his veins. He returned to the Radcliffe Camera, hoping to catch a glimpse of the action Daniel had hinted at earlier.

The moment he stepped inside, he felt it—the charge in the air. Low whispers, heavy breathing, and the unmistakable sound of slick skin against skin.

His cock stirred, hardening instantly as he spotted a cluster of men in the corner—pants around their ankles, hands stroking in unison.

"Fuck," Alex breathed, his pulse racing.

Without hesitation, he stepped closer, unzipping his jeans and letting them drop. His thick, aching cock sprang free, already dripping with need.

THE TEMPTATION OF ALEX

Meanwhile, Alex couldn't shake the restless energy coursing through his veins. He returned to the Radcliffe Camera, hoping to catch a glimpse of the action Daniel had hinted at earlier.

The moment he stepped inside, he felt it—the charge in the air. Low whispers, heavy breathing, and the unmistakable sound of slick skin against skin.

His cock stirred, hardening instantly as he spotted a cluster of men in the corner—pants around their ankles, hands stroking in unison.

"Fuck," Alex breathed, his pulse racing.

Without hesitation, he stepped closer, unzipping his jeans and letting them drop. His thick, aching cock sprang free, already dripping with need.

Eyes turned toward him as he stroked himself, their gazes adding fuel to the fire.

"You want to watch?" one man asked, smirking as he pumped his cock.

"No," Alex growled. **"I want to join."**

He moved closer, letting his shoulder brush against another man's as they stroked side by side. The heat of bare skin sent shivers through him.

The man turned, his body thick with muscle, and locked eyes with Alex.

"Let me taste you," he said, sinking to his knees.

Alex groaned as hot, wet lips wrapped around him. He thrust deeper, gripping the man's hair and fucking his mouth with growing intensity.

"Take it. Take it all."

EXPLORING NEW TERRITORY

Another man stepped forward, pulling Alex's free hand to his cock. Alex stroked him, savoring the weight and heat as their bodies pressed together.

"You're fucking gorgeous," the stranger whispered, biting Alex's neck.

The mix of mouths, tongues, and hands overwhelmed him, the intensity of it all pushing him toward the edge.

"I'm gonna cum," Alex panted, his hips snapping forward.

"Do it," the man said, pulling off just in time to let Alex spill onto his chest, the hot streaks glistening in the dim light.

The men collapsed into a tangled heap, panting and sweat-slicked.

Alex looked around, taking in the sight of spent bodies and satisfied grins.

"That was... unbelievable," he said, brushing damp hair from his forehead.

"Welcome to the club," someone replied, smirking as he zipped up his pants.

But Alex wasn't done. Not yet.

"Maybe next time," he said, pulling his jeans back up, **"I'll bring a friend."**

. . .

The Promise of More

As he walked out into the cool Oxford night, Alex couldn't stop replaying the experience in his mind—the heat, the hunger, the way his body had been consumed by pure need.

The Radcliffe Camera had revealed its secrets, and Alex wasn't about to stop exploring.

He checked his phone. A text from Daniel lit up the screen.

> Tell me you went back.

Alex grinned as he typed his response.

> You won't believe what I found. Meet me there tomorrow night.

And just like that, the promise of more—more pleasure, more risk, more exploration—set his pulse racing all over again.

3
SEX IN THE GARDEN

Oxford's Secret Passions

In the heart of Oxford, where intellect sparked and passions simmered, the cobbled streets and towering spires shielded more than scholarly debates and ancient manuscripts. Beneath the polished veneer of academia, the university throbbed with sexual energy—a hidden world where hot students and commanding professors collided in a dance of knowledge and desire.

The students were walking contradictions—intelligent yet reckless, polished yet primal. They moved through the hallowed halls with an easy confidence, their lean, athletic bodies honed by rowing on the river and rugby on the fields. Their voices were rich and resonant, carrying echoes of youthful arrogance and unspeakable hunger. Beneath their tailored blazers and fitted trousers, their bodies promised raw power and untamed passion, waiting to be unleashed.

The professors, on the other hand, embodied power and authority. Their tailored suits concealed broad shoulders and muscled chests, sculpted by morning swims and late-night gym sessions.

Their polished shoes and carefully chosen ties hinted at control, but their eyes betrayed darker appetites. They exuded dominance, their voices deep and deliberate, leaving students hanging on every word—and every lingering glance.

The magnetic pull between them was impossible to ignore. An undercurrent of tension crackled in lecture halls and spilled into dimly lit offices and shadowed gardens.

Late-night tutorials often became lessons in seduction—the flicker of candlelight and the glow of desk lamps illuminating stolen kisses and whispered confessions. A professor's hand might linger on a student's shoulder too long, a subtle invitation to cross boundaries. In the stillness of libraries and dormitories, bookshelves and desks became stages for forbidden trysts—buttons undone, ties loosened, and mouths exploring secrets never meant to be shared.

Walls absorbed the sounds of bodies colliding, breath hitching, and moans echoing off stained glass windows. Professors bent students over mahogany desks, pinning them down as discipline turned into desire. Students knelt before their mentors, eager to worship the men who held power over them.

Oxford's legacy wasn't just one of academic brilliance—it was also a sanctuary for forbidden pleasure. Hidden corners, candlelit studies, and ivy-covered courtyards became playgrounds for desire, where minds expanded, and bodies surrendered.

Day after day, night after night, these men explored the depths of both knowledge and lust. Each encounter blurred the line between teacher and student, between dominance and submission. The university became more than an institution—it became a stage for seduction, a theater where intellect met passion in a dance that would forever change the course of history. And perhaps even more importantly, their own lives.

. . .

The Garden of Desire

Daniel and Alex, two of Oxford's hottest students, slipped through the ivy-covered archway into the abandoned garden, their hearts pounding with anticipation. Overgrown vines twisted around crumbling stone walls, and shattered windows cast eerie beams of moonlight across the mossy ground. The space felt alive —charged with secrets and shadows, a sanctuary where passion could run wild.

Daniel's eyes darkened as he stepped closer, his fingers brushing Alex's jaw.

"I've wanted this all day," Daniel murmured, his lips grazing Alex's ear.

"Then take it," Alex growled, his voice low and desperate.

Their mouths collided—hot, wet, and hungry. Teeth clashed, tongues tangled, and their hard cocks ground together through layers of denim, the friction sparking electric heat. The cool night air did nothing to cool their fire as Daniel shoved Alex against the moss-covered wall, hands already working to unbuckle his belt.

On His Knees

Daniel dropped to his knees, tugging down Alex's jeans and briefs in one swift motion. Alex's cock sprang free, thick and hard, already dripping with need.

"Fuck—don't stop," Alex hissed, his fingers tangling in Daniel's hair as he thrust forward, feeding his cock into Daniel's eager mouth.

Daniel moaned around him, the vibrations sending shudders through Alex's body. He took him deep, hollowing his cheeks and working him with lips and tongue, savoring the salty slickness that coated his tongue.

"You're so fucking good at this," Alex groaned, his hips bucking as Daniel sucked harder, faster.

Daniel pulled back just long enough to growl, **"Cum for me."**

Alex's body tensed, his cock pulsing as he exploded down Daniel's throat. Daniel swallowed every drop, licking his lips before standing and pressing his mouth against Alex's in a hungry kiss, letting him taste himself.

Pinned and Taken

Daniel spun Alex around and pushed him against the wall, his fingers roughly pulling his ass apart.

"Do it. Fuck me," Alex begged, spreading his legs and arching his back.

Daniel spat into his hand, slicking his cock before pressing the head against Alex's tight hole.

"You ready?" Daniel growled, the tip pushing just inside.

"Yes—please!" Alex panted, desperation dripping from every word.

Daniel thrust forward, burying himself to the hilt with a guttural moan. Alex cried out, his fingers scraping at the stone wall as Daniel gripped his hips and set a brutal rhythm. Skin slapped against skin, echoing through the garden, raw and unrestrained.

"You like being used like this?" Daniel snarled, slamming deeper, his cock stretching Alex with every thrust.

"Yes—fuck, yes!" Alex gasped, pushing back to meet every stroke.

. . .

Claimed Completely

Daniel reached around and wrapped his fingers around Alex's cock, stroking him in time with each thrust.

"Cum again," Daniel demanded. **"I want to feel you lose it while I'm inside you."**

Alex whimpered, his body trembling as another orgasm ripped through him. Cum shot against the wall, streaking the moss-covered stone, and the sight of it pushed Daniel over the edge.

With a final, punishing thrust, Daniel groaned, his cock pulsing as he filled Alex with hot, sticky ropes of cum. He stayed buried inside him, his breath ragged as the aftershocks of release rippled through his body.

The Afterglow

They collapsed together onto the mossy ground, their sweat-slicked bodies tangled. Daniel ran his fingers down Alex's spine, his lips grazing the back of his neck.

"You're fucking incredible," Daniel whispered.

"So are you," Alex replied, turning his head for a lazy kiss.

The garden around them was silent once more, save for the rustling of leaves and the distant hoot of an owl. But Daniel knew this night wasn't the end—it was only the beginning.

The Library of Lust

Daniel's hunger didn't end in the garden. Later that night, the Bodleian Library called to him—a cathedral of knowledge by day, but by night, a temple of secrets and sin. Shadows stretched long across the towering shelves, the faint scent of old paper and polished wood mingling with something darker—something primal.

As he wandered deeper into the stacks, Daniel froze.

Men—young and old, students and scholars—stood in clusters, their pants pooled around their ankles, hands working slick, hard cocks. Low moans echoed off the marble floors, mingling with the faint creak of wood and the rhythmic slap of skin.

Daniel's cock stiffened instantly, pressing painfully against his jeans as he drank in the sight—muscular thighs, broad shoulders, sweat-slicked chests, and dripping shafts pumping with abandon.

"Fuck," he muttered, his fingers already unzipping his pants.

He stepped into the circle, dropping his jeans and briefs in one swift motion. His thick cock sprang free, and heads turned. Eyes locked on him—hungry, predatory—and Daniel felt the heat of their gazes fuel his arousal.

Exposed and Worshipped

"You're beautiful," a tall, dark-haired man whispered, stepping closer, his own cock glistening with pre-cum.

Daniel smirked, pumping harder. **"You want it?"**

The man dropped to his knees, eyes filled with lust as he leaned in and wrapped his lips around Daniel's cock. The heat of his mouth was instant, wet, and greedy, his tongue teasing the sensitive head before sliding down the shaft.

Daniel groaned, thrusting forward, forcing the man to take more.

"That's it. Suck it. Take it deep."

A second man stepped behind him, pressing close—bare chest against Daniel's back—and slipped a hand down to spread his ass.

"You're tight," the stranger murmured, teasing Daniel's hole with slick fingers. **"Let me stretch you open."**

Daniel gasped as one finger pushed inside, followed by another, scissoring him apart. The stretch burned, but he pushed back, craving more.

"Fuck—don't stop."

The man's fingers curled, stroking Daniel's prostate, sending waves of pleasure through him as the kneeling man swallowed him deeper, sucking harder, moaning around his shaft.

DOUBLE THE PLEASURE

Daniel's knees threatened to give out as he was used from both ends, the dual sensations overwhelming him—wet heat surrounding his cock and slick fingers fucking him open.

"You're so fucking hot like this," the man behind him growled, spreading him wider and pushing deeper.

The intensity built, pressure coiling tighter and tighter as Daniel's moans grew louder.

"I'm gonna cum," he panted, thrusting hard into the man's mouth while rocking back onto the fingers stretching him.

"Do it," the man behind him urged, pushing deeper. **"Let them see you lose control."**

With a guttural cry, Daniel came hard, spilling down the kneeling man's throat in thick, hot spurts. The man moaned as he swallowed every drop, licking his lips before looking up at Daniel with hunger still burning in his eyes.

· · ·

The Afterglow and the Promise of More

Daniel staggered back, his breath ragged, his body trembling as he wiped sweat from his brow. The men surrounding him watched with admiration and lust, still stroking themselves as they waited for their own release.

He pulled up his jeans, the damp fabric sticking to his skin as he turned and caught the eye of the man who had opened him with his fingers.

"Next time, you're going to fuck me," Daniel said, his voice low and commanding.

"I'll make sure you can't walk afterward," the man replied with a smirk.

As Daniel stepped out into the night air, his body still humming with satisfaction, he knew this was only the beginning. Oxford's secrets ran deep, and he intended to uncover every last one—one forbidden encounter at a time.

4
DANIEL'S WORLD UNVEILED

Morning Rituals

Daniel stretched his arms above his head, letting out a contented sigh as the warm sunlight filtered through the thin curtains of his college dorm. His lean, muscular frame flexed as he sat up, the sheets falling away to reveal the bulge in his boxers— already thick, hard, and straining against the fabric. He glanced at the clock. Past seven. Time to start the day.

Padding barefoot across the wooden floor, he flipped on the kettle before returning to sit on the edge of his bed. His eyes dropped to the massive outline in his underwear, and a smirk tugged at his lips. His morning wood was as dependable as the rising sun, a daily reminder of the energy and hunger that coursed through him.

"Looks like you're ready to start the day, too," he murmured, palming the heat radiating through the fabric.

He slid his boxers down, freeing his cock—thick, veined, and already slick with precum. Wrapping his fingers around the shaft, he gave it a slow, teasing stroke, savoring the sensation.

· · ·

THE FANTASY BEGINS

Daniel leaned back, closing his eyes and letting his mind wander. He imagined himself somewhere darker—an underground sex club filled with towering, muscular men in leather harnesses and tight jockstraps. Their eyes devoured him, hungry and possessive, their bodies hard and ready.

"**Come here,**" one of them growled in his imagination, pulling Daniel by the hips and pinning him against a wall.

The fantasy deepened as Daniel's strokes quickened. He imagined their hands roaming his body—rough fingers pinching his nipples, another man's tongue trailing down his abs. In his mind, they surrounded him, bodies pressing close, cocks grinding against him.

"**You're ours tonight,**" a voice whispered, and Daniel's breath hitched.

His grip tightened, his free hand sliding down to cup his balls and tug them gently.

"**Fuck—yes,**" he groaned, his hips bucking as he imagined being bent over, his wrists bound, and his ass stretched by one man while another fed his cock into Daniel's mouth.

The image of being taken—used, filled—pushed him closer to the edge. His muscles tensed, his abs flexing as heat surged through his body.

"**I'm gonna cum,**" Daniel panted, his strokes turning frantic.

He gritted his teeth as the climax ripped through him, hot ropes of cum spilling over his fingers and dripping onto his stomach and thighs. His body shuddered with aftershocks, the pleasure lingering as he let out a low, satisfied groan.

. . .

THE AFTERGLOW

Opening his eyes, Daniel looked down at the mess he'd made, a smug grin spreading across his face.

"Perfect start," he muttered, reaching for tissues to clean himself up.

Still flushed from his orgasm, he rose and padded to the bathroom for a quick shower. The hot water cascaded over his body, rinsing away the evidence of his morning indulgence, but the fantasy still lingered in his mind.

Back in his room, Daniel dressed with care. He chose a crisp white shirt that clung to his toned chest and tailored trousers that framed his thick thighs and barely contained his bulge. A spritz of cologne added the finishing touch—a masculine scent that hinted at leather and musk.

"Ready to make them stare," he said, smirking at his reflection before stepping out into the world, already craving whatever forbidden pleasures the day might bring.

THE RITUAL OF PERFECTION

Daniel stepped into the steamy communal shower, the hot water cascading down his broad shoulders and sculpted chest. He lathered up with a rich, citrus-scented body wash, the suds clinging to his muscles as his hands roamed over every inch of his toned frame. He lingered on his pecs, rolling his nipples between soapy fingers before trailing down to his abs, his cock already semi-hard from the attention.

"You're insatiable," he muttered, giving himself a quick squeeze before rinsing off.

By the time he stepped out, towel wrapped low around his hips, the hall was deserted—though he wouldn't have minded if someone caught a glimpse of him dripping wet and hard. Back in his room, Daniel took his time selecting the day's outfit—a crisp white shirt that clung to his chest and tailored trousers that hugged his thighs. He smirked as he adjusted himself, making sure the thick outline of his cock was impossible to miss.

A spritz of cologne and a quick tousle of his dark hair completed the look. He caught his reflection in the mirror—blue eyes sharp, jawline chiseled, body exuding power and sex.

"Perfect," he murmured before heading out.

COMMANDING ATTENTION

The courtyard buzzed with morning activity as Daniel strode through the crowd, his magnetic presence turning heads. He flashed his signature smirk, greeting classmates and professors alike. Their eyes lingered on the unmistakable bulge in his trousers, some discreetly glancing away while others let their stares linger.

"Morning, Daniel," one of the tutors called out, his voice faltering as his gaze drifted downward.

"Good morning, Professor," Daniel replied, slowing just enough to let the man drink him in before moving on.

He loved the effect he had—how their words stumbled and their cheeks flushed. He didn't just turn heads; he left people breathless.

Settling into his lecture on Shakespearean literature, Daniel leaned back in his chair, crossing one leg over the other. The position drew even more attention to the prominent ridge in his trousers. He caught the professor's eyes flicker downward mid-sentence, and Daniel smirked, feigning innocence as he shifted to make the bulge even more obvious.

"Is something distracting you, Professor?" he asked, his voice smooth and deliberate.

The professor stammered but recovered quickly.

"Not at all, Daniel. Please continue your analysis."

THE WEIGHT OF DESIRE

Throughout the day, Daniel thrived on the tension he created. Conversations about literature and philosophy often veered off-course as his presence overwhelmed those around him. Students hung on his every word, their gazes betraying the thoughts racing through their minds. Professors, despite their attempts at professionalism, couldn't stop themselves from sneaking glances.

"You have quite the... presence, Daniel," one tutor had admitted during a private meeting.

"I've been told," Daniel replied, spreading his legs wider as he leaned back in the chair.

The tutor's eyes flickered downward, lingering far too long before stammering out the rest of the lesson. Daniel loved it—loved knowing he could reduce even the most composed men to trembling messes without lifting a finger.

DOMINANCE IN EVERY STEP

As evening approached, Daniel returned to his dorm, his cock already stirring again as he replayed the day's encounters. He stripped down, letting his trousers and briefs pool around his ankles before flopping onto the bed.

Gripping his thick shaft, he stroked himself slowly, savoring the memories—professors fumbling their words, students blushing, and one particularly eager tutor whose gaze had lingered far too long.

"You'd drop to your knees if I told you to," Daniel growled, imagining the tutor's lips wrapped around his cock.

His strokes quickened, his breath hitching as he pictured gripping the man's hair and pushing deeper, using his mouth until tears streamed down his face.

"Take it all," Daniel groaned, his hips bucking as he spilled hot, sticky ropes of cum across his abs.

Panting, Daniel wiped himself clean, still tingling from the release. But even as he lay back, muscles relaxing, his cock twitched—already stirring at the thought of what tomorrow might bring.

He knew he was special—not just because of his mind or charisma, but because of something deeper, something primal. His cock wasn't just an asset; it was a weapon. A tool of power, dominance, and seduction.

"Tomorrow," Daniel whispered to himself, smirking as he closed his eyes, **"I'll make them beg for more."**

The Seduction of Knowledge

Daniel's love for literature was as profound as it was insatiable. He devoured books with an almost obsessive hunger, losing himself in the intoxicating worlds crafted by words. Through the pages, he discovered reflections of his own desires—dark, forbidden, and impossible to ignore.

Oscar Wilde's *The Picture of Dorian Gray* captivated him like no other. The tale of beauty corrupted, of secrets hidden behind elegance, resonated with Daniel's own cravings—for pleasure, control, and surrender. As he read, Wilde's lush prose stirred something deeper, igniting a fire that burned low in his belly and throbbed in his cock.

His erection strained against his trousers as his eyes devoured the words. The flickering candlelight and the shadows in the corners of the room made it feel as though Wilde's ghost was watching him, urging him to give in to his most dangerous impulses.

"Fuck," Daniel whispered under his breath, shifting in his seat as the pressure against his groin grew unbearable.

The Tutor's Temptation

The door creaked open, and Daniel barely had time to adjust himself before Professor Harding stepped inside. The older man carried himself with authority—tall, broad-shouldered, and dressed in a fitted tweed suit that emphasized his power. His sharp eyes locked on Daniel, lingering just long enough to make the student's pulse quicken.

"Still hard at work, I see," Harding said, his voice low and deliberate.

Daniel's breath caught as Harding approached, stopping just behind him. The professor's hand rested lightly on his shoulder, his thumb tracing slow circles.

"It's good to see you so focused," Harding murmured, leaning down until his lips were close to Daniel's ear.

Daniel swallowed hard, his cock twitching under the weight of Harding's touch.

"I can't put it down," Daniel replied, his voice steady but soft.

"Neither can I," Harding said, his gaze drifting lower.

· · ·

Corruption Unveiled

Daniel turned another page, deliberately leaning back so Harding could see the bulge pressing against his trousers. The professor's breath hitched, his hand sliding down to squeeze Daniel's shoulder more firmly.

Daniel shifted again, his hips lifting just enough to push his erection against the desk's edge, making the outline even more obvious.

"I see you're... deeply engaged," Harding whispered, his tone dark and knowing.

"You could say that."

Harding moved closer, his thigh pressing against Daniel's back as he pretended to study the text. Daniel felt the professor's cock hardening through his trousers, pressing insistently against him.

"Reading Wilde always gets me thinking about... temptation," Harding said, his hand trailing down Daniel's arm. **"What about you?"**

"Temptation's impossible to resist," Daniel replied, shifting so that Harding could feel his body respond.

The Release of Power

Harding leaned in further, his cock grinding against Daniel's back as his hand drifted lower, fingers brushing the edge of Daniel's belt.

"Keep reading," Harding ordered, his voice tight with lust.

Daniel obeyed, his voice trembling slightly as he continued reciting Wilde's words about corruption and beauty. Harding's hips pressed harder, his breathing quickening as his erection rubbed against Daniel.

"You're so fucking hot," Harding growled, his hand dipping lower to brush against Daniel's bulge.

Daniel tilted his hips forward, offering himself.

"I want to hear you lose control," Daniel murmured, smirking as Harding's breath hitched.

The professor's hand tightened, and Daniel felt the unmistakable pulse of Harding's cock as he climaxed, muffling a groan into Daniel's neck.

"Fuck," Harding hissed, his hips stuttering as his release soaked through his trousers.

THE SATISFACTION OF DOMINANCE

Daniel sat still, smirking as Harding tried to compose himself, straightening his jacket and adjusting his tie.

"Clean yourself up," Daniel said, his voice low and commanding.

Harding glanced down at the mess in his pants, flustered but obedient.

"And next time," Daniel added, **"bring me something filthier to read."**

As Harding hurried out of the room, Daniel leaned back, his cock still throbbing in his trousers. He ran his fingers along the bulge, knowing he could make the professor beg next time.

Literature had always aroused Daniel, but the men who taught it were proving to be his favorite lesson of all. With a satisfied grin, he returned to his book, already imagining the next chapter in his education.

. . .

THE ALLURE OF FORBIDDEN KNOWLEDGE

Daniel's heart raced as he replayed the illicit encounters he'd shared with his tutors. There was something intoxicating about the forbidden—something that spoke to the darkest corners of his soul. He had always craved older, experienced men who could teach him more than literature—men who could unlock his raw, primal desires and push him past the boundaries of propriety.

Professor Sinclair had been the first. A brilliant scholar with sharp features and an authoritative presence, Sinclair exuded dominance. Daniel had caught the older man's eye in a freshman seminar on Victorian literature, and it hadn't taken long for their academic relationship to spiral into something far more physical.

"You've got a rare talent, Daniel," Sinclair had said after one class, gesturing for him to sit at his desk.

The praise made Daniel's cock twitch as he felt Sinclair's gaze rake over him—his broad shoulders straining against his shirt, his muscular thighs pressing against his trousers, and most of all, the outline of his massive cock barely contained by the fabric.

Without a word, Sinclair's hands slid over Daniel's knees, his touch firm and deliberate. Daniel shivered, the thrill of being claimed flooding his veins as the professor's fingers trailed higher.

"You don't mind staying after class for some... private tutoring, do you?" Sinclair murmured, his voice dark and commanding.

Daniel's breath caught.

"Not at all, sir."

From that day forward, their meetings burned with urgency. Sinclair would sit behind his desk, legs spread, stroking himself openly as he spoke about Shakespeare's sonnets and the erotic undertones of Greek mythology. Daniel would watch in fascination as the professor's cock swelled in his hand, a bead of precum glistening at the tip.

"You like watching, don't you?" Sinclair had growled one evening, his voice thick with lust.

"Yes, sir," Daniel admitted, his own cock painfully hard in his trousers.

"Then get on your knees."

THE POWER OF SUBMISSION

Daniel obeyed, sinking to the floor and staring up at Sinclair's cock—thick, veined, and dripping. He licked his lips before wrapping them around the head, savoring the salty taste as Sinclair groaned and buried his hands in Daniel's hair.

"Good boy," Sinclair whispered, pushing deeper, his hips rocking as he fucked Daniel's mouth. **"Take it all."**

Daniel gagged but didn't stop, letting the older man use him until his jaw ached and tears pricked the corners of his eyes. He loved the weight of Sinclair's cock on his tongue, the sounds of his grunts echoing through the office, and the thrill of knowing anyone could walk in at any moment.

"I'm close," Sinclair growled, pulling out and stroking himself furiously.

Daniel opened his mouth, ready. Sinclair groaned as he came, ropes of hot cum streaking across Daniel's lips and chin.

"Clean yourself up," Sinclair said, his voice rough.

Daniel grinned as he wiped his mouth with the back of his hand, licking his lips and savoring the taste.

. . .

The Legacy of Desire

Those secret meetings with Sinclair had left their mark, fueling Daniel's hunger for dominance and submission and making him acutely aware of his power over men. He strode through the courtyard with confidence, his wet hair glistening in the sunlight and his blue eyes smoldering as he greeted students and professors alike.

Eyes lingered on him wherever he went—especially on the prominent bulge that strained against his tailored trousers. His cock was impossible to hide, a permanent reminder of his raw masculinity, and he had no intention of concealing it.

Tutors struggled to keep their focus during tutorials, their eyes drifting to his crotch as they stammered through explanations.

"You're... quite the presence, Daniel," one professor had muttered, his voice trembling.

"So I've been told," Daniel replied, leaning back and spreading his legs just enough to make the outline even more obvious.

Commanding Attention

Daniel's effect on others was undeniable. Classmates hung on his every word during debates, professors faltered mid-sentence, and strangers in the library couldn't help but sneak glances as he walked past.

"You make it impossible to focus," one student confessed during a late-night study session.

"That's the point," Daniel said with a smirk.

He reveled in their stares, in the hunger he could see simmering just below the surface. He knew his body was as much a weapon as his mind—and he wielded both with precision.

· · ·

A Life of Seduction

As evening fell, Daniel returned to his dorm, his cock already hard again as he thought about the day's encounters. Stripping down, he lay back on his bed and stroked himself slowly, imagining Sinclair bending him over the desk again or one of his classmates on their knees, begging to taste him.

"Take it," Daniel whispered, his grip tightening as the fantasy consumed him.

His body tensed as the orgasm hit, cum shooting across his abs in thick, hot streams. He exhaled shakily, already craving more.

"Tomorrow," he murmured, **"I'll make them beg for it."**

He drifted to sleep, his cock still semi-hard, already dreaming of the men he'd dominate and seduce next.

5
TEACHER'S PET

T he Café Encounter

"Excuse me," the handsome young man said nervously as he slid into the seat across from Daniel without asking, his boldness betrayed by the flush in his cheeks. His eyes flickered downward—briefly, but noticeably—lingering on the obvious bulge stretching the fabric of Daniel's tight pants before darting back up. "I couldn't help but notice ... well ... you know ..."

Daniel smirked, leaning back in his chair and spreading his legs slightly, daring the boy's eyes to wander again.

"Notice what?" he asked, voice low and teasing.

The young man swallowed hard, clearly struggling with his words. "Your ... um ... cock."

Daniel raised an eyebrow, clearly amused but intrigued. "Yes? What about it?"

The boy's blush deepened, but he didn't look away this time. Instead, his gaze locked onto Daniel's with growing determination.

"It just seems ... so big ... and ... well ... impressive." He paused, then stumbled through the rest. "I just wanted to say if you ever needed someone to—uh—help out ... to get off ... or fuck ... I'm ready and willing."

"Thank you," Daniel said, chuckling softly. "I take pride in my assets." He shifted slightly in his chair, the movement deliberate, letting the outline of his massive cock press even more prominently against the fabric.

"Would you like to see more?" Daniel teased, one hand drifting toward the zipper. "Or should we head somewhere more private?"

Behind Closed Doors

Daniel's pulse quickened as he shut the door to his dorm room, locking it behind the eager young man who had followed him without hesitation.

"Strip for me," Daniel commanded, his voice rough with desire.

The young man hesitated, then began peeling away his clothes, slow and deliberate. When the last piece hit the floor, Daniel drank in the sight—lean, toned muscles, a light dusting of hair, and an already hard cock standing proudly.

"Damn," Daniel muttered. "You're even hotter than I imagined."

He unzipped his pants, letting them drop. His cock sprang free, thick, veined, and dripping pre-come. The young man's eyes widened, and his mouth fell open.

"Touch it," Daniel ordered, grabbing the boy's wrist and guiding his trembling hand to the base. "Feel how hard I am for you."

. . .

THE FIRST TOUCH

The boy obeyed, wrapping his fingers around Daniel's shaft and stroking slowly. Daniel groaned, throwing his head back against the wall as the pleasure built.

"That's it," he moaned. "But I need more than just your hand."

He pulled the boy close, their lips crashing together in a heated kiss. Hands explored freely—grabbing, squeezing, stroking—as they pressed against each other, hungry and desperate.

Breaking the kiss, Daniel shoved the boy back onto the bed, climbing on top of him. His cock slid between the boy's cheeks, teasing his hole as he pinned him down.

"Are you ready for me?" Daniel asked, voice dark with lust.

The young man nodded frantically, spreading his legs wider.

"Good," Daniel growled. "Because I don't hold back."

TAKING CONTROL

Daniel spat into his hand, slicking up his cock before pressing the tip against the boy's tight entrance.

"Relax," he whispered. "Let me stretch you open."

He pushed forward slowly, the head popping inside, and the boy gasped—half pain, half pleasure.

"You're so fucking tight," Daniel groaned, inching deeper. "But you can take it, can't you?"

"Yes," the boy moaned. "Please—fuck me."

Daniel started slow, rocking his hips, letting the boy adjust to his size. But it wasn't long before lust overtook him, and he began to

WHISPERS IN THE RADCLIFFE CAMERA

thrust harder, faster, the sound of skin slapping echoing through the room.

"You like this?" Daniel growled, gripping the boy's hips and pounding into him. **"You like being stretched wide and filled?"**

"Yes! Fuck—yes!" the boy cried, his own cock leaking pre-come onto the sheets as Daniel drove deeper, hitting every spot that made him tremble.

THE CLIMAX

Daniel felt the tension building, the heat coiling low in his stomach.

"I'm close," he warned. **"Touch yourself while I fuck you."**

The boy obeyed, fisting his cock in time with Daniel's thrusts. It didn't take long—Daniel groaned, driving deep one last time as he spilled inside, his cock pulsing hard. The boy followed moments later, moaning as he came, his cum splattering across his stomach.

Daniel collapsed beside him, panting.

"Fuck," the boy whispered, still catching his breath. **"That was ... incredible."**

Daniel grinned, already thinking about round two.

"You're not leaving yet," he said. **"We're just getting started."**

THE ART OF DESIRE

Daniel stood back from the canvas, his brush frozen mid-stroke. The painting captured a raw intensity—a half-naked man sprawled across a chaise lounge, muscles taut and glistening, frozen in a moment of ecstasy. It wasn't just art; it was desire made visible.

The door creaked open, and Daniel turned. One of his teammates stepped inside, still in his football gear, sweat clinging to his skin. Tall, broad-shouldered, and effortlessly masculine, he oozed confidence—but his eyes betrayed curiosity as they lingered on the painting.

"Hey," the teammate said, leaning casually against the doorframe. **"I didn't know you painted."**

Daniel smirked, lowering his brush. **"Yeah. It's how I get out what's inside."**

The guy stepped closer, their shoulders brushing as he studied the painting.

"These are ... incredible," he murmured, his fingers tracing the painted muscles. **"You're really talented."**

Daniel held his gaze, letting the tension stretch. **"I could use someone like you as a model. You up for it?"**

"Hell yeah," the guy said, his grin daring Daniel to take things further.

STRIPPED BARE

Daniel peeled off his shirt, revealing his toned chest.

"You're jacked, dude."

"You're not so bad yourself." Daniel stepped closer, his fingers grazing the edge of the guy's jersey. **"Why don't you lose this?"**

The jersey hit the floor, and Daniel's breath caught. Chiseled pecs, sculpted abs, and a thin sheen of sweat that begged to be licked off.

"**Damn,**" Daniel said, running his hands over the smooth, hard ridges. "**You're built like a statue.**"

He leaned in, his lips brushing the guy's neck, trailing lower to tease his nipples.

"**Shit, bro,**" the guy moaned. "**That feels so good.**"

Down to Business

Daniel dropped to his knees, pressing his face against the bulge in the guy's pants.

"**You're already hard for me, aren't you?**" he teased, inhaling the scent of sweat and musk.

"**Fuck, yes,**" the guy panted. "**Please, man. Don't stop.**"

Daniel tugged down his jeans and boxers in one motion, freeing the thick, throbbing cock that sprang out.

"**Damn,**" he said, licking his lips. "**You're perfect.**"

Grabbing the base, he licked along the shaft, swirling his tongue around the head before taking it deep into his mouth.

"**Fuck, Daniel! That's so good!**"

Daniel sucked harder, his lips gliding up and down as his fingers explored the guy's muscular thighs. He let his teeth graze the sensitive skin just enough to make him gasp.

"**Don't tease me,**" the guy groaned. "**I need more!**"

Dominance and Submission

Daniel pulled off with a wet pop and wiped his lips.

"**You'll get more,**" he promised. "**But first, get on the bed.**"

The guy obeyed, lying back and spreading his legs as Daniel climbed on top, pinning him down. Their cocks brushed, the friction sparking moans from both of them.

"You're mine now," Daniel growled, grinding his hips.

"Fuck me," the guy begged.

Daniel grabbed a bottle of lube from the nightstand, slicking his fingers before pressing one inside.

"So tight," he murmured, watching the guy writhe beneath him. He added a second finger, stretching him wider. **"You're gonna feel amazing wrapped around me."**

"Please—do it," the guy panted.

THE FINAL STRETCH

Daniel slicked himself up and pressed the head of his cock against the guy's entrance.

"Ready?"

"God, yes."

Daniel pushed in slowly, savoring the stretch as the guy moaned beneath him.

"You're taking me so well," he said, gripping his hips and driving deeper. **"You feel incredible."**

He picked up speed, each thrust hitting the guy's prostate and pulling cries of pleasure from his lips.

"Fuck, don't stop!"

"I'm not stopping until I've filled you up," Daniel growled.

He pounded harder, sweat dripping down his chest as their bodies collided in rhythm.

. . .

THE CLIMAX

"**I'm so close!**" the guy moaned.

"**Come for me,**" Daniel ordered, wrapping a hand around his cock and stroking him in sync with his thrusts.

The guy tensed, his body shaking as he came hard, ropes of cum splattering across his abs. Daniel followed seconds later, burying himself deep as he filled the guy, his own groans echoing through the room.

They collapsed together, bodies slick with sweat and satisfaction.

"**Fuck,**" the guy whispered. "**That was ... insane.**"

Daniel grinned, already thinking about round two.

"**We're not done yet,**" he said.

BEGGING FOR RELEASE

"**Fuck,**" he gasped. "**Oh, fuck. Yes. Please.**"

Daniel's tongue dragged slowly along the underside of his friend's cock, tasting the salty pre-come already leaking from the tip. He wrapped his lips around the swollen head and sucked, hollowing his cheeks before letting it pop free, wet and glistening. His hands roamed lower, fingers teasing over sensitive skin, caressing the tight sac and brushing lower, just enough to make the young man's hips jerk.

He felt the tension coiling in his friend's body—the flex of his thighs, the quiver in his abs, the shaky breath that betrayed just how close he was.

"**Please,**" the young man whimpered, voice thick with desperation. "**I need... I need to come. Please, let me come.**"

Daniel looked up, his lips curling into a wicked smile. Slowly and deliberately, he licked the tip again.

"**Not yet,**" he whispered, his voice low and commanding. "**I want you to feel this. Really feel it.**"

The Edge of Control

He gripped the base of his friend's cock tighter, stroking with a slick rhythm while his tongue teased the head—slow, then fast, then slow again—driving him wild. His free hand slid down, fingers grazing the sensitive skin behind his balls, pressing lightly, threatening to go further but always stopping just short.

"**Please!**" the young man gasped, his voice breaking. "**I can't—I can't take it. Please!**"

Daniel chuckled darkly, his breath hot against the slick skin. He loved seeing him like this—spread out, trembling, utterly wrecked. He took his cock back into his mouth, lips stretched wide as he swallowed him deep.

Daniel sucked hard and fast, hollowing his cheeks, his tongue pressing and swirling as the young man's moans turned into incoherent cries. He felt him tense, every muscle locking up before he shattered—hips bucking, body shaking as his orgasm ripped through him.

Hot, thick streams spilled into Daniel's mouth, and he swallowed greedily, not stopping until he'd taken every last drop. He pulled back slowly, letting his tongue drag along the length one last time, savoring the shudder that followed.

"**Fuck,**" the young man panted, his voice raw. "**That was... incredible.**"

. . .

ONE MORE ROUND

Daniel grinned, wiping the corner of his mouth as he knelt between his friend's spread legs. His cock was still rock hard, slick with pre-come, the tip brushing against the young man's inner thigh.

"Glad you liked it," he said, his voice dripping with mischief. **"But we're not done yet."**

He wrapped his fingers around his own length, stroking slowly as he leaned closer, letting the heat of his body press against his friend's skin.

"There's still one more thing I want from you," he murmured. **"Think you can handle it?"**

The young man's eyes dropped to Daniel's cock—thick, veined, and dripping with pre-come. His lips parted as if he were in awe, but instead of hesitating, he grinned and leaned in, letting his tongue flick across the swollen head.

"Fuck," Daniel groaned, his fingers threading through the young man's hair. **"That's it. Suck it."**

The young man opened wider, taking more of Daniel's cock into his mouth. His lips stretched, and his tongue swirled, teasing the sensitive underside as he bobbed his head, eager and determined.

"You like this, don't you?" Daniel murmured, gripping his hair tighter. **"You love how I feel in your mouth."**

The young man moaned in response, the vibration making Daniel shudder. He pushed deeper, making the boy gag slightly before pulling back just enough to let him catch his breath.

"You're such a good boy," Daniel praised. **"But now I need more."**

. . .

Begging for It

Daniel pulled the young man up, kissing him hard as he led him to the bed. He pushed him down onto his back, spreading his legs wide.

"I want you to feel every inch of me," Daniel growled, trailing kisses down the young man's body until he reached his thighs. He licked and nipped at the sensitive skin, making him squirm.

"Please," the young man moaned, writhing beneath him. **"I need it. Fuck me. Please."**

Daniel pressed the head of his cock against the tight, waiting hole, teasing him with shallow thrusts.

"You're not ready yet," Daniel said, smirking. **"Not until you beg for it."**

"I'm begging! Please, Daniel—fuck me. I need it so bad!"

Daniel didn't make him wait any longer. With one steady push, he sank inside, groaning as the young man's body stretched to take him.

"Fuck, you're tight," Daniel hissed, gripping the boy's hips. **"You feel so fucking good."**

The young man moaned, his body arching as he adjusted to the size.

"More," he begged, his voice breathless. **"Don't hold back."**

Daniel started slow, rolling his hips and grinding deep, but his control didn't last long. The heat, the slick tightness around his cock, drove him wild. His thrusts quickened, harder and deeper, the sound of skin slapping echoing through the room.

"You're mine," Daniel growled, pinning him down. **"You're gonna take every inch of me."**

"Yes! Fuck—yes!" the young man cried, his nails digging into Daniel's back.

Riding the Edge

Daniel pushed the young man's legs higher, folding him back as he pounded harder. He angled his thrusts, hitting his sweet spot with every stroke, making him cry out louder.

"You like being fucked like this?" Daniel demanded, sweat dripping from his chest.

"Yes—fuck—don't stop!"

Daniel reached down, grabbing the young man's cock and stroking it in time with his thrusts.

"Come for me," he ordered. **"I want to feel you lose control."**

The young man's body tensed, his cries turning to broken moans as he came hard, spilling across his stomach and Daniel's hand.

"Fuck, yes," Daniel groaned, driving deeper as his own orgasm hit. He buried himself inside, pumping his release into the young man's trembling body.

After the High

Daniel collapsed on top of him, their bodies slick with sweat and cum.

"Holy shit," the young man panted. **"That was ... incredible."**

Daniel smirked, brushing his lips against the boy's neck. **"You're mine now,"** he whispered. **"And we're just getting started."**

From that moment on, Daniel knew that art would never be enough to capture his desires. He'd need to live them—boldly, unapologetically—and this was only the beginning.

6

FOOTBALL FREEBALLING

Commanding the Field

Daniel's heart pounded as he stepped onto the football field, the cool air brushing against his exposed skin beneath his loose shorts. His massive cock swung freely, a beast barely contained, and he knew the others noticed. The glances weren't subtle—admiring stares, envious glares, and lingering looks that trailed his every move.

"Damn, Daniel," one of the players muttered as he passed. **"How the hell do you run with that thing swinging around?"**

Daniel smirked, rolling his shoulders. **"Confidence and control."** He winked. **"You should try it sometime."**

As practice began, Daniel's body collided with his teammates in the scrum, the rough contact sending shivers of arousal through him. Every tackle, every push, and grind against sweat-slicked muscles made his cock pulse harder. He bit back a moan, but his shorts betrayed him—several inches of thick, veined shaft peeking out from the hem.

· · ·

Rough Play

Daniel squared off against Jake, the team's most aggressive player —a wall of muscle and testosterone with a cocky smirk to match. Their eyes locked, and the tension between them shifted from competitive to primal.

"You think you can take me?" Jake growled, stepping closer, his chest heaving.

"Why don't you find out?" Daniel shot back, his voice low and dripping with challenge.

Without hesitation, Daniel's hand shot out, cupping Jake's bulge through his shorts. The thick heat beneath his palm made his cock throb.

Jake groaned, grabbing Daniel's cock through the thin fabric, and squeezing hard enough to make Daniel gasp.

"Fuck, man," Jake hissed, his eyes dark with hunger. **"You're a fucking beast."**

Daniel didn't hesitate. In one swift motion, he yanked down both their shorts, letting their cocks spring free—thick, hard, and glistening with precum.

"Look at us," Daniel murmured, wrapping one strong hand around both shafts and stroking them together. **"Two fucking gods."**

The Team's Temptation

The rest of the team froze, eyes locked on the sight of Daniel and Jake standing naked in the middle of the field, their cocks pressed together, precum smearing between them.

"You gonna just watch?" Daniel taunted, licking his lips. **"Or are you gonna join us?"**

The challenge hung in the air, but Jake didn't wait for an answer. He lunged forward, crushing his mouth against Daniel's in a hungry kiss. Their tongues tangled, teeth nipping, as hands roamed over sweat-slick muscles.

"Fuck me," Jake panted, breaking the kiss. **"Right here. Right now."**

Daniel shoved him down onto the grass, forcing his legs apart. He spit into his hand, slicking up his cock as he knelt between Jake's spread thighs.

"You're gonna take it all," Daniel growled, pressing the thick head of his cock against Jake's tight hole. **"You ready for this?"**

"Hell yes. Give it to me."

Daniel pushed in slowly, savoring the stretch as Jake's body opened around him. The tight heat made Daniel groan, and he gripped Jake's hips, holding him still as he buried himself deeper.

"Fuck, you're tight," Daniel hissed. **"You feel so fucking good."**

Jake moaned, his muscles tensing, his fingers digging into the grass.

"More—don't hold back."

Unleashed

Daniel didn't need any more encouragement. He slammed his hips forward, driving into Jake with deep, punishing thrusts.

"You like that?" Daniel growled, sweat dripping down his chest. **"You like getting fucked in front of the whole team?"**

"Yes! Fuck—yes!" Jake cried, arching his back, his cock leaking onto his stomach.

The sound of skin slapping filled the air as Daniel pounded harder, the others watching in stunned silence, their hands moving over their own cocks as they stroked to the filthy scene.

"You're mine," Daniel snarled, grabbing Jake's cock and jerking it in time with his thrusts. **"Now fucking come for me."**

Jake's whole body tensed as he let out a ragged moan, spurting ropes of cum across his abs. The sight pushed Daniel over the edge.

"Fuck, take it all," he groaned, slamming in one last time and burying himself deep as his cock pulsed, filling Jake with hot, thick cum.

The team erupted into cheers, some still stroking themselves as Daniel pulled out and stood over Jake's spent body.

"Who's next?" Daniel asked, his cock still slick and hard.

Jake grinned up at him. **"I'll take round two when you're ready."**

Daniel smirked, licking his lips.

"You better be ready, because I'm just getting started."

DOMINATING THE GAME

Daniel didn't hold back. He slammed into Jake with relentless force, each thrust sending shockwaves through his body. The wet slap of skin against skin filled the air, mingling with Jake's ragged moans and the heavy breaths of the other players, who stood around them, stroking their cocks as they watched.

"You like this?" Daniel growled, gripping Jake's hips tighter. **"You like getting fucked in front of the whole team? Being my little slut out here on the field?"**

"Yes! Fuck yes!" Jake cried out, his body rocking helplessly beneath Daniel's relentless thrusts.

Daniel leaned in, his breath hot against Jake's ear. **"You're mine,"** he growled. **"Now come for me. Show them how much you fucking love this."**

Daniel reached down, wrapping his fist around Jake's cock, stroking it in perfect rhythm with his pounding hips. Jake's moans turned to desperate cries as his body tightened.

"Fuck! I'm—oh god—I'm coming!" Jake gasped, his cock erupting in thick ropes of cum that splattered across his abs.

The sight pushed Daniel over the edge. With a guttural groan, he drove deep, burying himself inside Jake as he came, filling him with hot, pulsing spurts.

Daniel didn't stop until he'd drained every last drop, then slowly pulled out, leaving Jake panting and spent on the grass.

"Good boy," Daniel said, slapping Jake's ass. **"You took me like a fucking champ."**

THE NEXT CHALLENGER

The rest of the team didn't move, their eyes locked on Daniel's glistening cock—still hard, still leaking.

"Who's next?" Daniel demanded, licking his lips. **"I'm not done yet."**

The players exchanged glances, their cocks still throbbing, until Ethan—the dark-haired artist and Daniel's occasional lover—stepped forward.

"I think it's my turn," Ethan said, his voice thick with lust as he stripped off his gear.

Daniel's eyes darkened with hunger as he looked Ethan up and down, admiring the sculpted lines of his chest and the thick cock already dripping pre-come.

"Get on your knees," Daniel ordered.

Ethan dropped without hesitation, his eyes fixed on Daniel's cock as he licked his lips.

A New Challenge

Daniel grabbed Ethan's hair, guiding his mouth toward his cock.

"OPEN UP," HE COMMANDED. "AND DON'T STOP UNTIL I say so."

Ethan obeyed, his lips wrapping around the slick head as Daniel pushed deep, making him gag before pulling back slightly.

"That's it," Daniel groaned. "Take it. Make me proud."

The other players moved in closer, stroking themselves as they watched Ethan work, his head bobbing up and down while Daniel thrust into his throat.

Daniel grinned. This wasn't just a game—it was a show of dominance, a display of raw power and lust that left the entire team aching to be next.

"You're gonna swallow every drop," Daniel growled. "And then I'm gonna bend you over and fuck you right here in front of everyone."

Ethan moaned around his cock, and Daniel smirked.

"Hope you're ready," Daniel said, his voice thick with promise. "Because I don't play fair."

. . .

THE INNER CIRCLE

Daniel's network of lovers extended far beyond the football team. Ethan had been his first—an artist who saw beauty in Daniel's body and worshipped it like a muse. Their connection started in the dorm showers, where Ethan had dropped the soap just to sneak a longer look at Daniel's cock.

Jake, the muscle-bound linebacker, had been his most intense partner—always eager to prove his strength, whether on the field or in the bedroom. And there were others—musicians, scholars, and wrestlers—each drawn to Daniel's magnetism and his insatiable hunger for control and pleasure.

Every encounter added to Daniel's legend, whispered about in locker rooms and dorms, fueling fantasies and jealousies. He wasn't just a player—he was a force of nature, a god among men who demanded worship and devotion.

THE AFTERMATH

Daniel stood on the field, sweaty and spent, but far from satisfied.

"Practice is over," he announced, zipping up his shorts. **"But tonight? Tonight, we finish what we started."**

The team erupted into cheers, already anticipating the next round. Daniel grinned—his legacy wasn't just about football. It was about power, dominance, and the raw, unfiltered pleasure that came from giving in to desire.

End of Passage.

THE NETWORK OF DESIRE

Daniel's network of lovers was as vast as it was discreet—a carefully curated collection of men who satisfied his insatiable cravings and fed his appetite for control, submission, and raw passion. Jake, with his brute strength and willingness to be dominated, and Ethan, the dark-haired artist who worshipped Daniel's body like it was a masterpiece, were just two of many who had entered his orbit.

Each man brought something different to the table—strength, creativity, vulnerability, or raw, animalistic lust—and Daniel took his time exploring them all. Some wanted to be tamed, others to tame him, and Daniel thrived on the variety. But there were rules.

No one crossed paths. No group encounters. Every connection was intensely private—one-on-one sessions where secrets were whispered, boundaries were tested, and desires were unleashed without fear of judgment.

"You're perfect," one of his lovers had said breathlessly after being pinned down and fucked so hard he could barely stand. **"No one else could make me feel this way."**

But Daniel knew better. He wasn't perfect. He was a man built for pleasure but haunted by the ache for something more.

The Weight of Loneliness

As the sun dipped below the horizon, Daniel sat alone in his dorm room, staring out the window. His reflection stared back at him—a body sculpted by years of athletic training, a face that turned heads, and a cock that had left men trembling and begging for more. But beneath the confidence and swagger, there was a hollowness that gnawed at him.

He ran a hand down his chest, tracing the ridges of muscle, but it wasn't enough. No matter how many men he took or how many moans he pulled from their lips, the emptiness remained.

"You're incredible," Ethan had whispered one night after collapsing onto Daniel's bed, his body slick with sweat and cum. **"I'd do anything for you."**

Daniel had smiled, but it didn't reach his eyes. Ethan had meant the words, but Daniel knew the truth—he wasn't enough. Not for Ethan. Not for anyone.

CHASING CONNECTION

He replayed the encounters in his mind—the way Jake had begged to be fucked harder, the way Ethan had dropped to his knees without hesitation, and the countless others who had passed through his door, seeking pleasure and release. They all wanted him, but none had truly seen him.

Daniel craved more than bodies pressed together in heated desperation. He wanted intimacy—the kind that couldn't be faked or fucked into existence.

He imagined what it might feel like to have someone who wasn't intimidated by his size or defined by the sex they shared. Someone who could look past the raw physicality and see the man underneath—the one who dreamed of being touched not just for pleasure but for love.

DREAMS OF SOMETHING MORE

As night fell, Daniel stretched out on his bed, staring up at the ceiling. The ache inside him grew, pulsing like a second heartbeat. He closed his eyes and let his fantasies take over—visions of a man who didn't flinch at his hunger, who didn't just take what he offered but gave back in equal measure.

In his dream, there were no rules, no carefully curated arrangements—just two men tangled in sheets, their bodies and souls laid bare. He imagined strong hands holding him, not just for pleasure but for comfort. Lips that kissed not only his cock but every inch of him, as if each part mattered just as much as the rest.

"I see you," the dream lover whispered. **"All of you."**

Daniel moaned softly in his sleep, his body responding to the fantasy even as his heart ached for it to be real.

Waking Desires

When he woke, the room was dark, the sheets damp with sweat and the lingering scent of arousal. Daniel ran a hand through his hair, staring at the ceiling.

He knew better than to believe in dreams. His life was built on dominance, control, and carefully guarded boundaries. But as he lay there, the echoes of the dream lingered, refusing to fade.

For the first time in a long time, Daniel allowed himself to hope— that somewhere out there was someone who could give him what he needed.

Not just submission. Not just admiration.

Love.

The Library Encounter

Daniel's pulse quickened as he wandered through the towering shelves of the campus library, his eyes discreetly tracking Oliver— the new stud on campus. Tall, broad-shouldered, and impossibly handsome, Oliver exuded confidence even as he browsed the shelves with laser focus.

Daniel had heard the rumors—Oliver was more than just a pretty face. He was a bookworm, someone who appreciated the power of words as much as the weight of a barbell. It was rare to find someone who stirred Daniel's body and mind in equal measure, and the thought of exploring both possibilities made his cock twitch.

Gathering his nerve, Daniel stepped closer.

"Hey," he said softly, his voice steady despite the fire burning in his chest. **"I didn't know you liked coming to the library."**

Oliver looked up, startled but smiling. **"Yeah, it's one of my favorite places on campus. There's just something about being surrounded by all these books that makes me feel alive."**

Daniel's lips curled into a smile. **"Mind if I join you? I could use some company."**

Oliver's eyes scanned the quiet aisles before he nodded. **"Sure thing. I could use someone to talk to as well."**

A Shared Connection

They settled into a secluded corner surrounded by books—thick tomes and leather-bound volumes that seemed to echo the gravity of their conversation.

Words flowed effortlessly. Favorite authors, guilty pleasures, and literary fantasies—each topic drew them closer. Daniel watched Oliver's lips move, mesmerized by the way he spoke with passion and precision.

Oliver's fingers idly traced the spines of the books beside him, and Daniel couldn't stop his imagination from drifting. He pictured those same fingers trailing down his chest, tugging at his waistband, and stroking his cock until he was trembling.

"You're easy to talk to," Oliver said suddenly, pulling Daniel back to reality.

"So are you," Daniel replied, letting his eyes linger on Oliver's mouth for just a second too long.

UNSPOKEN DESIRE

The conversation slowed, replaced by lingering looks and subtle touches. Oliver's knee brushed Daniel's thigh under the table, and neither man moved away.

Daniel felt his cock stir, pressing against the confines of his jeans. He shifted slightly, wondering if Oliver had noticed—and hoping he had.

"You okay?" Oliver asked, his voice softer now.

"Yeah," Daniel said, clearing his throat. **"Just... distracted."**

Oliver smirked. **"By what?"**

Daniel leaned in closer, his voice dropping to a husky whisper. **"By you."**

Oliver's eyes darkened, his breath hitching.

"What about me?" he asked, the challenge clear in his voice.

BREAKING BOUNDARIES

Daniel reached out, brushing his fingers along Oliver's wrist, testing the waters.

"You make it hard to focus," he said. **"And not just on books."**

Oliver's lips parted slightly, and Daniel didn't wait for permission. He leaned in, capturing Oliver's mouth in a slow, deliberate kiss.

Oliver responded instantly, his tongue sliding against Daniel's as he reached up to grip his hair.

"**Fuck,**" Oliver whispered when they broke apart. "**I've been thinking about this since the moment I saw you.**"

"**Then let's stop thinking.**" Daniel stood, tugging Oliver to his feet and leading him deeper into the stacks.

They were hidden now, surrounded by books but exposed to their own hunger. Daniel pushed Oliver against the shelves, pinning him in place as their mouths crashed together again—hotter, rougher this time.

Daniel's hands roamed freely, sliding under Oliver's shirt to feel the hard ridges of his abs.

"**You've been holding out on me,**" Daniel growled, sucking on Oliver's neck.

"**Not anymore.**"

Oliver reached down, unzipping Daniel's jeans and pulling out his cock.

"**Jesus,**" Oliver muttered, staring at its size. "**How the fuck is this even real?**"

"**You're about to find out.**"

Daniel spun him around, pressing his chest against the shelves. He yanked Oliver's jeans down, exposing his firm ass.

"**Spread your legs.**"

Oliver obeyed, and Daniel spit into his hand, slicking up his cock before pressing the head against Oliver's tight hole.

"**You ready for this?**"

"**Fuck yes,**" Oliver moaned. "**Do it.**"

. . .

Claiming His Prize

Daniel pushed in slowly, savoring the stretch as Oliver gasped.

"God, you're so fucking tight," Daniel hissed, gripping Oliver's hips and pulling him back onto his cock.

Oliver moaned, his hands bracing against the shelves as Daniel started to thrust—slow at first, then faster, harder, until the sound of skin slapping echoed through the aisle.

"You like being fucked like this?" Daniel growled.

"Yes! Don't stop!" Oliver begged, pushing back against him.

Daniel reached around, stroking Oliver's cock in rhythm with his thrusts.

"Come for me," he demanded.

Oliver's body tensed, and he let out a strangled cry as he came, spurting hot ropes of cum onto the floor. The sight sent Daniel over the edge.

"Fuck, take it," he groaned, burying himself deep as he filled Oliver with hot spurts of cum.

A New Chapter

They stayed there for a moment, panting and trembling before Daniel pulled out, his cock still dripping.

"We should do this again," Oliver said, turning to face him with a grin.

"Count on it," Daniel replied, pulling him into another kiss.

As they cleaned up and straightened their clothes, Daniel couldn't stop smiling. For the first time in a long time, he felt like this wasn't just another conquest. It was the beginning of something more—something worth exploring.

AWAKENING DESIRE

The fantasy was so vivid that Daniel could almost feel Oliver's touch—the soft glide of fingers tracing the length of his cock, sending shivers rippling through him. He imagined Oliver's lips wrapped around him, wet and hot, sucking with a hunger that left Daniel breathless and desperate for more.

His cock throbbed, the bulge in his pants impossible to hide. Daniel glanced down, his pulse quickening as he looked back up to find Oliver still lost in thought, oblivious—or so it seemed. But Daniel knew there was more to this than unspoken longing. The tension simmering between them was real, and it begged to be unleashed.

Taking a steadying breath, Daniel decided to risk it. He reached out, placing a hand firmly on Oliver's thigh. The warmth of his skin burned through the fabric, and Oliver froze, looking up in surprise.

"I can't stop thinking about you," Daniel whispered, his voice low and heavy with need.

Oliver's eyes widened before he gave a slow, eager nod.

"Me neither."

BEHIND CLOSED DOORS

The library was quiet, but the pounding of Daniel's heart echoed in his ears as he led Oliver to one of the private study rooms.

The tension built quickly, their voices dropping to hushed whispers as they shared fantasies—stories of past encounters and confessions about what they wanted to do to each other. Words turned to touches—subtle at first but quickly escalating as their desire took control.

Daniel pressed Oliver against the wall, his hands sliding under his shirt, feeling the smooth, taut muscles beneath.

"You're fucking gorgeous," Daniel murmured, tugging Oliver's shirt over his head.

"So are you."

Their lips crashed together, tongues tangling in a messy, heated kiss. Daniel's hands roamed lower, unbuckling Oliver's jeans and shoving them down to reveal the hardness straining against his underwear.

"Take it off," Daniel growled, stepping back just enough to watch Oliver strip completely.

When Oliver stood naked before him, his skin flushed and glistening, Daniel's breath caught.

"Damn," Daniel said, stepping closer. **"You're perfect."**

Oliver's cock twitched, and Daniel dropped to his knees without hesitation, his mouth enveloping the thick shaft in one smooth motion.

"Fuck!" Oliver moaned, his hands flying to Daniel's hair, gripping tightly. **"That feels so good."**

Daniel sucked greedily, his tongue swirling around the head before sliding lower, taking him deep. He let his teeth scrape lightly, just enough to make Oliver gasp and thrust forward.

"You taste so fucking good," Daniel groaned, stroking the base with one hand as his other teased Oliver's balls.

"Don't stop," Oliver begged, his voice breaking. **"I'm so close."**

But Daniel did stop. He stood, licking his lips as he pushed Oliver back onto the table.

Taking Control

"**Spread your legs,**" Daniel ordered, pulling a condom and lube from his bag.

Oliver obeyed, spreading wide as Daniel slicked himself up, the thick head of his cock pressing against Oliver's tight hole.

"**You ready for me?**"

"**Yes. Fuck me.**"

Daniel pushed in slowly, savoring the stretch as Oliver's body opened for him.

"**Shit, you're tight,**" Daniel groaned, gripping Oliver's thighs as he sank deeper.

Oliver moaned, his fingers digging into Daniel's back. "**More—don't hold back.**"

Daniel didn't. He thrust harder, faster, their bodies slamming together in a frenzy of sweat and heat.

"**You like this?**" Daniel growled. "**You like being fucked like this?**"

"**Yes! Fuck—don't stop!**"

Daniel reached between them, stroking Oliver's cock in rhythm with his thrusts.

"**Come for me,**" Daniel demanded. "**Show me how much you want this.**"

Oliver let out a strangled moan, his body tensing as he exploded, cum splattering across his stomach. The sight pushed Daniel over the edge, and with one final thrust, he buried himself deep, filling the condom with thick spurts of cum.

Panting, they collapsed against each other, their bodies slick and trembling.

"Holy shit," Oliver muttered, looking up at Daniel with a dazed smile.

"You're mine now," Daniel said, brushing his lips against Oliver's. **"And this is just the beginning."**

BEYOND DESIRE

Their connection didn't fade when the heat cooled. Over the following weeks, Daniel and Oliver explored not only their bodies but each other's minds. They spent long nights talking about books, art, and life—conversations that always seemed to end with tangled sheets and breathless moans.

Daniel painted Oliver, capturing every detail of his body—the curve of his spine, the cut of his abs, the hunger in his eyes. Each brushstroke felt like a declaration, not just of lust but of something deeper.

"You see me," Oliver had whispered one night, tracing Daniel's jaw. **"All of me."**

And Daniel had smiled, knowing it was true.

As months turned into years, Daniel's art flourished. His paintings of Oliver—raw, passionate, and vulnerable—became his most celebrated work. But for Daniel, it wasn't just about the art. It was about the man who had inspired it, the man who had shown him that love and lust didn't have to be separate, and that the deepest connections often started with desire.

7

YOUR ZIPPER'S OPEN, DUDE

Disciplined Desires

The sun had barely risen as Oliver stepped out of his college residence, the crisp morning air biting against his skin. But inside, heat churned—a hunger that no amount of cold could suppress. His days were governed by two rituals: mornings spent sculpting his body in the gym and afternoons lost in the quiet sanctity of the Bodleian Library.

Oliver thrived in both spaces—surrounded by sweat and iron in one, by ancient texts and hushed reverence in the other. The contrast fueled him. The raw, physical exertion grounded him, while the mental discipline of research elevated him. Both worlds satisfied a part of him, but neither was enough.

His hunger demanded more. And Oliver had no qualms about feeding it.

TOUCHING THE PAST

Oliver's fingers glided over the spines of ancient books, tracing the worn leather covers with the same reverence he reserved for sculpted flesh. He let the smell of ink and paper wash over him, stirring something primal. These books had survived centuries, yet they yielded to his touch—a thought that made his cock stir.

As he lingered in the shadows of the stacks, Oliver's mind wandered. He pictured himself pressed against these shelves; his briefs shoved down as another man claimed him. He imagined the sharp scrape of old bindings against his back, the heat of rough hands gripping his thighs, spreading him wide.

The library wasn't just a refuge for his mind—it was foreplay for the darker cravings that simmered just beneath the surface.

By noon, Oliver traded the library's whispered promises for the growls and grunts of the weight room. Sweat clung to his skin as he pressed heavier and harder, pushing his body to the limit. He thrived in this environment of testosterone and unspoken competition, but it wasn't just the weights that caught his attention.

Across the room, a tall man with broad shoulders and carved abs had Oliver's full focus. Their eyes locked during a set of deadlifts, and the heat between them was as palpable as the musk filling the air.

"Nice form," Oliver said, approaching confidently.

"Thanks. You too," the man replied, his gaze dropping briefly to the outline of Oliver's cock pressing against his shorts.

"We should work out together sometime."

"Why wait?"

Numbers were exchanged, but their intentions didn't need spelling out.

LOCKER ROOM HEAT

As night fell, Oliver returned to the gym—this time dressed for seduction. Tight black briefs hugged his muscular frame, leaving nothing to the imagination. When his new companion arrived, shirtless and wearing only boxer briefs, Oliver felt his cock stir immediately.

"Fuck, you look good," Oliver growled, stepping closer.

"So do you."

They wasted no time, their bodies colliding in a heated embrace as they pushed into the secluded locker room showers. Oliver's hands roamed, sliding over slick skin, exploring ridges of muscle and hard flesh.

"You've been teasing me all day," Oliver muttered, gripping the man's thick cock through his briefs.

"And now you're gonna take it," the man growled, shoving Oliver against the cold tile wall.

Oliver moaned as the man pinned him, their mouths crashing together in a hungry kiss. Teeth scraped, tongues tangled, and hands tore away the last barriers of fabric.

"Get on your knees," the man ordered, and Oliver obeyed, dropping to the wet floor.

He wrapped his lips around the thick, dripping cock, swallowing it down until his nose pressed against the man's trimmed pubes.

"Fuck, that's good," the man groaned, gripping Oliver's hair and thrusting deep. **"You like choking on my cock, don't you?"**

Oliver moaned around the shaft, his cock leaking pre-come as he let the man use his throat.

"That's it," the man growled. **"You're such a fucking slut for this."**

When the man pulled out, Oliver gasped for air, but before he could stand, he was spun around and bent over the bench.

"You ready for me?" the man asked, pressing the thick head of his cock against Oliver's tight hole.

"Do it," Oliver begged.

OWNED AND USED

The man pushed in slowly at first, stretching Oliver open.

"Fuck, you're tight," he hissed, grabbing Oliver's hips and slamming deeper.

Oliver moaned loudly, his cock grinding against the cold bench with every thrust.

"You like being fucked like this?" the man growled, pounding harder.

"Yes! Use me!" Oliver cried, pushing back to take more.

The locker room echoed with the sounds of skin slapping and heavy breathing as the man drove into Oliver, claiming him without restraint.

"I'm gonna fill you up," the man growled, and Oliver groaned in response.

When the man came, burying himself deep, Oliver's cock pulsed, shooting thick ropes of cum onto the floor without even being touched.

Panting, they collapsed onto the bench, sweat dripping from their bodies.

"Fuck, that was hot," the man said, still catching his breath.

Oliver grinned. **"You should see what I'm like when I'm not holding back."**

"Guess I'll have to come back for more."

Oliver leaned in, biting the man's lip. **"Count on it."**

THE SCHOLAR'S OBSESSION

Oliver's heart raced as he stepped into the Bodleian Library, the scent of aged leather and parchment thick in the air. His fingers itched to trace the spines of the newly arrived manuscripts—rare treasures from a monastery in Italy. Each book held secrets, stories, and mysteries, and Oliver longed to devour them.

But today, his hunger wasn't just for knowledge.

Professor Michaelson awaited him. Brilliant, accomplished, and undeniably hot, Michaelson was a walking fantasy—lean muscles hidden beneath crisp shirts and piercing blue eyes that seemed to see straight through Oliver. He wasn't just a mentor. He was temptation personified.

Oliver's cock stirred at the thought of spending the afternoon alone with him, and he couldn't help but wonder—would their intellectual connection ever spill over into something more primal?

CROSSING BOUNDARIES

"So," Michaelson said, leaning back in his chair, one leg casually crossed over the other. **"What have you brought me today?"**

Oliver swallowed hard and laid the manuscript on the table. Flipping through the delicate pages, highlighting passages and interpretations, he felt Michaelson's gaze—not on the text but on him.

"These are incredible," Michaelson said, brushing his fingertips along the page. **"You're clearly passionate about this."**

Oliver blushed but pressed on, gesturing animatedly as their conversation deepened. The air between them grew thick—not just with ideas, but with something unspoken, electric.

When Oliver finally paused, his voice hoarse, he became acutely aware of his damp clothes clinging to his body. The sudden shift in focus made him bold.

Without a word, he tugged off his shirt, revealing his toned chest and abs. His shorts followed, leaving him in nothing but a black jockstrap that left very little to the imagination.

Michaelson's eyebrow lifted, but he didn't speak. His gaze lingered, tracing every ridge of Oliver's muscles before settling on the obvious bulge pressing against the thin fabric.

"Would it offend you if I continued our tutorial like this?" Oliver asked, his voice soft but steady. He adjusted his semi-hard cock through the jockstrap, his fingers lingering. **"I'm sorry, sir. I'm just so hot and sweaty. But if it's too distracting, I'll get dressed again."**

Michaelson smirked, clearly enjoying the show.

"No," he said, his voice lower now. **"I don't mind at all."**

Encouraged, Oliver stepped closer, leaning in as if to point out a detail in the manuscript but pressing his thigh against Michaelson's.

"You seem distracted, Professor."

"And you seem to like it," Michaelson replied, his hand drifting to Oliver's hip.

. . .

Claiming the Student

Michaelson's fingers grazed the curve of Oliver's ass, tracing the edge of the jockstrap.

"You're playing a dangerous game," Michaelson whispered, leaning closer.

"Maybe I want to lose," Oliver shot back, grabbing Michaelson's tie and pulling him in for a kiss.

Their mouths collided, tongues tangling as Michaelson pushed Oliver back against the bookshelf. Books rattled, but neither man cared.

Michaelson's hands roamed, sliding over Oliver's pecs and down to his bulge, squeezing it firmly through the fabric.

"You've been teasing me all day," Michaelson growled. **"Now it's my turn."**

He dropped to his knees, pulling the jockstrap down to free Oliver's cock.

"Goddamn," Michaelson muttered before taking him deep into his mouth.

Oliver groaned, his fingers tangling in Michaelson's hair as the professor worked him over—licking, sucking, and teasing the sensitive tip.

"Fuck, you're good at this," Oliver moaned. **"But I need more."**

Power Shift

Michaelson stood, wiping his mouth before pushing Oliver down onto the table.

"On your knees," he ordered, unzipping his trousers.

Oliver obeyed, his own cock dripping as Michaelson pressed the thick head of his cock against Oliver's lips.

"Open up."

Oliver took him eagerly, his throat stretching as Michaelson thrust deeper.

"Such a good boy," Michaelson groaned, guiding Oliver's head. **"Take it all."**

When Michaelson pulled out, Oliver gasped, but before he could speak, he was bent over the desk.

"You're mine now," Michaelson growled, slicking his cock with spit and pressing it against Oliver's tight hole.

"Please, sir," Oliver begged, pushing back. **"I need it."**

Michaelson pushed in slowly, stretching him wide.

"Fuck, you're tight," he groaned, gripping Oliver's hips as he sank deeper.

"Harder," Oliver demanded, and Michaelson obliged, slamming into him with deep, punishing thrusts.

The sound of skin slapping and ragged breaths filled the room.

"You like being used like this?" Michaelson growled.

"Yes! Don't stop!"

Michaelson reached around, stroking Oliver's cock in rhythm with his thrusts.

"Come for me," he ordered.

Oliver cried out as he exploded, ropes of cum splattering across the desk. Moments later, Michaelson buried himself deep, groaning as he filled the condom with thick spurts of cum.

. . .

AFTERMATH

Breathless, they collapsed against each other.

"I should punish you for that distraction," Michaelson teased, running his fingers through Oliver's hair.

"Maybe next time, sir," Oliver replied, smirking. **"If you can handle me."**

Michaelson leaned down, biting Oliver's neck.

"Oh, I can handle you."

As Oliver dressed, his legs still shaky, he knew this was only the beginning. Their connection—intellectual, physical, and filthy—was far from over.

THE MAGNETIC STRANGER

Oliver strolled confidently across the central green, his muscular frame commanding attention. The sun caught the sharp angles of his jaw and the ripple of muscle beneath his fitted shirt, but it was more than his looks that turned heads—it was the air of mystery that clung to him like a second skin.

Students lounging on the grass paused mid-conversation to watch him, their eyes trailing his every step. But one man stood out.

Daniel.

Tall, broad-shouldered, and ruggedly handsome, Daniel's shaggy brown hair framed piercing blue eyes that locked onto Oliver like a predator sizing up prey. Oliver smirked, already intrigued by the undone zipper of Daniel's jeans—teasing a glimpse of thick pubic hair that hinted at what lay beneath.

Oliver didn't hesitate. He approached, his voice low and deliberate.

"Hello," he said, extending his hand. **"I'm Oliver."**

Daniel hesitated, then took Oliver's hand. Their fingers intertwined, and the jolt that passed between them was electric.

"I'm Daniel."

They stood there, eyes locked, the tension palpable.

"I couldn't help but notice your... unique fashion choice," Oliver teased, nodding toward Daniel's unzipped jeans.

Daniel blushed but held his ground. **"I guess I just forgot to zip up this morning."**

Oliver smirked and leaned in, his fingers grazing the waistband of Daniel's jeans.

"Seems like you've got something worth showing off."

Breaking Boundaries

Before Daniel could respond, Oliver tugged gently on his jeans, exposing more of the thick, wiry hair beneath. Daniel's breath hitched, but he didn't resist.

Oliver pushed further, slipping his hand inside, his fingers brushing against the heat of Daniel's cock through the fabric of his underwear.

"You like this?" Oliver whispered, his voice thick with desire.

Daniel groaned softly, his hips pushing forward. **"Fuck, yes."**

Oliver's fingers found Daniel's piss slit, teasing it through the thin fabric, and Daniel's knees buckled slightly.

"I want to taste you," Oliver murmured, leaning in to capture Daniel's lips in a hungry kiss.

Daniel moaned into his mouth, his hands tangling in Oliver's hair, pulling him closer as their tongues tangled in a heated, messy rhythm.

Oliver broke the kiss, his lips slick and swollen.

"Come with me," he said hoarsely, tugging Daniel's hand as he led him toward a secluded bench under the trees.

They sat down, their bodies pressed close as their hands roamed freely.

Oliver teased Daniel's nipples, pinching them until he moaned, while Daniel's fingers found the bulge in Oliver's jockstrap, pulling it aside to free his stiff, dripping cock.

"You're fucking huge," Daniel whispered, wrapping his fingers around it and stroking slowly.

"You can handle it," Oliver replied, his hips thrusting into Daniel's grip.

Surrender and Control

Daniel pushed Oliver back against the bench and knelt between his legs, his tongue darting out to lick the pre-cum glistening at the tip.

"Fuck," Oliver groaned, gripping Daniel's hair. **"Suck it."**

Daniel obeyed, taking the head into his mouth and swirling his tongue around it. He worked his way down the shaft, letting it slide deeper until his nose brushed against Oliver's trimmed pubes.

GRIFF HOLLAND

"**Good boy,**" Oliver moaned, thrusting gently. "**Take it deeper.**"

Daniel gagged slightly but didn't stop, hollowing his cheeks and sucking harder as Oliver's grip tightened in his hair.

"**You love this, don't you?**" Oliver growled.

Daniel nodded, moaning around the cock in his mouth.

"**You're gonna make me come, but first...**"

Oliver pushed Daniel onto the bench, pulling off his jeans completely to reveal a thick, throbbing cock already leaking pre-cum.

"**Fuck, you're perfect,**" Oliver said before taking Daniel into his mouth, sucking hungrily.

Daniel moaned, his hands gripping Oliver's head as he thrust deeper.

"**Don't stop,**" he begged. "**I'm so close.**"

Oliver pulled off just long enough to spit on Daniel's cock, stroking it firmly.

"**Come for me,**" he demanded, his tongue flicking against the head.

With a strangled cry, Daniel's cock erupted, hot streams coating Oliver's lips and tongue. Oliver swallowed eagerly, milking every drop as Daniel writhed beneath him.

"**Fuck, Oliver,**" Daniel gasped. "**That was...**"

Oliver wiped his mouth and grinned. "**We're not done yet.**"

The Aftermath

Still breathless, Oliver stood and pulled Daniel up, pinning him against the tree behind the bench.

84

"**I need more,**" Oliver growled, grinding his still-hard cock against Daniel's ass.

"**Take me,**" Daniel whispered, his voice raw.

Oliver didn't hesitate. He spit into his hand, slicking himself up before pressing the head against Daniel's tight entrance.

"**Relax,**" Oliver whispered. "**You're mine now.**"

He pushed in slowly, stretching Daniel open until he was buried to the hilt.

"**Fuck, you're so tight,**" Oliver groaned, gripping Daniel's hips.

Daniel moaned, pushing back. "**Harder.**"

Oliver obeyed, thrusting deep and hard, their moans echoing through the trees.

"**Come again for me,**" Oliver demanded, stroking Daniel's cock as he pounded into him.

With a cry, Daniel came again, his body trembling as Oliver followed, spilling deep inside him.

THE NEXT CHAPTER

They collapsed together, panting.

"**You're mine now,**" Oliver whispered, biting Daniel's neck.

"**And you're not getting rid of me,**" Daniel replied with a grin.

As they dressed, Oliver's gaze lingered on Daniel's flushed skin and swollen lips. This wasn't just a hookup. It was the start of something darker, deeper, and far more dangerous.

Just as Daniel's body tensed, ready to explode, Oliver pulled away abruptly, leaving him gasping and trembling with desperation.

"Not yet," Oliver whispered, his voice low and commanding as he stood and pulled Daniel to his feet. **"I have something else in mind."**

Without another word, Oliver grabbed Daniel's hand and led him deeper into the park, toward a towering tree that cast dappled shadows across the grass. He spun Daniel around and pressed him firmly against the rough bark, their bodies flush, their heat mingling.

"You trust me?" Oliver asked, his lips brushing Daniel's ear.

"Yes."

Oliver smirked and yanked down their jockstraps, leaving them naked except for their socks and sneakers.

Pinned and Exposed

Daniel groaned as Oliver pinned him harder against the tree, his muscular body dominating him.

"You've been teasing me all day," Oliver growled, wrapping his fist around Daniel's cock and stroking it slowly. **"Now it's my turn."**

Daniel's head fell back, his moans echoing through the trees as Oliver worked him with deliberate precision, alternating slow strokes with sudden, punishing squeezes.

Oliver leaned in, dragging his tongue along Daniel's neck before biting down gently.

"You like being manhandled, don't you?"

"Yes—fuck—don't stop," Daniel begged, pushing into Oliver's hand.

But Oliver did stop. He dropped to his knees, kissing down Daniel's chest and stomach, his tongue flicking over each sensitive inch.

"You taste so fucking good," Oliver murmured before taking Daniel's cock into his mouth.

Daniel cried out as Oliver sucked hungrily, his lips sliding up and down the shaft while his tongue teased the head.

"Fuck, Oliver," Daniel moaned, his hands tangling in Oliver's hair as he thrust deeper into his throat. **"You're gonna make me come."**

Oliver pulled back just enough to smirk. **"Not yet."**

He stood, wiping his mouth and grinning as he pushed Daniel toward a nearby bench.

"On your back," Oliver ordered, his voice rough with desire.

Daniel obeyed, his cock still slick from Oliver's mouth, standing hard and dripping. Oliver straddled him, their cocks rubbing together as he leaned in for another bruising kiss.

"You're mine now," Oliver whispered, grinding their bodies together.

THE EDGE OF CONTROL

Their hands explored one another, fingers trailing over sweat-slicked skin and gripping whatever they could reach.

Daniel moaned as Oliver wrapped his fingers around both their cocks, stroking them in unison, the friction driving them closer to the edge.

"You feel this?" Oliver growled. **"You're not coming until I say so."**

"**Please,**" Daniel panted. "**I need it—I need you.**"

Oliver pushed Daniel's legs apart and spat into his hand, slicking up his cock before pressing the head against Daniel's tight hole.

"**Ready?**"

"**God, yes.**"

Oliver pushed in slowly, savoring the stretch as Daniel moaned beneath him.

"**Fuck, you're so tight,**" Oliver groaned, gripping Daniel's hips as he sank deeper. "**You feel incredible.**"

CLAIMING THE PRIZE

Oliver didn't hold back. He thrust harder, deeper, the sound of skin slapping and desperate moans filling the air.

"**You like this?**" Oliver growled. "**You like being fucked out here where anyone could see?**"

"**Yes! Don't stop!**" Daniel begged, pushing back to meet each thrust.

Oliver reached between them, stroking Daniel's cock in rhythm with his movements.

"**Come for me,**" Oliver demanded. "**Now.**"

Daniel's body tensed, and with a strangled cry, he came hard, ropes of cum splattering his abs and Oliver's hand. The sight pushed Oliver over the edge, and with one final thrust, he buried himself deep, groaning as he filled Daniel with hot spurts of cum.

They collapsed against each other, panting and drenched in sweat.

"**Fuck,**" Daniel whispered, his voice shaky. "**That was...**"

Oliver smirked, brushing his lips against Daniel's. **"Just the beginning."**

The Mystery Deepens

Later, back in the library, Daniel found himself watching Oliver again, mesmerized as he moved through the rows of books with the same confidence he'd shown while pinning him against the tree.

Oliver ran his fingers reverently over the spines of ancient texts, his focus intense, but Daniel saw through it. He saw the heat that lingered just beneath the surface, the raw desire that had driven them together only hours earlier.

"You're staring," Oliver said suddenly, not even looking up.

Daniel blushed. **"Can you blame me?"**

Oliver smirked and turned, leaning casually against the shelves.

"You ready for round two?"

Daniel grinned. **"Always."**

As Oliver led him toward the restricted archives, Daniel's pulse quickened. Something told him this wouldn't just be another hookup. With Oliver, every moment promised to be an adventure —kinky, dirty, and completely unforgettable.

The Scholar's Temptation

Oliver's heart pounded as he stepped into the Bodleian Library, the scent of aged leather and ink wrapping around him like a lover's embrace. His fingers itched to trace the spines of the newly arrived manuscripts—ancient texts from a remote monastery in

Italy. Each page promised secrets, mysteries, and hidden desires waiting to be uncovered.

As he wandered deeper into the hallowed halls, Oliver felt the weight of history pressing in, the air thick with the scent of parchment and possibility. But today, his focus wasn't only on the manuscripts—his attention was drawn to something far more immediate and raw.

Daniel.

Seated at one of the heavy wooden tables, Daniel flipped through a worn volume of Shakespearean literature. His shaggy brown hair fell into his eyes, but it was the hint of exposed skin peeking above his unzipped jeans that made Oliver's cock stir.

BREAKING BOUNDARIES

Oliver approached slowly, his breath catching as Daniel looked up and met his gaze.

"You again," Daniel said, leaning back in his chair with a smirk. **"Couldn't stay away?"**

Oliver's lips curled into a sly smile. **"Not after the show you gave me earlier."**

Daniel's eyes darkened, and without hesitation, he reached down and pulled his zipper lower, spreading the piss slit of his boxer shorts wide. Thick pubic hair spilled out, and Oliver swallowed hard, heat pooling in his groin.

"I just wanted to remind you of the view you appreciated this morning," Daniel teased. **"Unless you've forgotten already?"**

Oliver's breath quickened. **"Trust me, it's burned into my memory."**

"**Then why aren't you helping me fix it?**" Daniel challenged, his voice low and rough.

Oliver stepped closer, his fingers grazing Daniel's waistband before pulling it down farther, exposing the thick root of his cock.

"**Fuck, you're hard already,**" Oliver whispered, leaning in. "**You're a fucking tease.**"

PUBLIC PASSION

Oliver didn't hesitate. He grabbed Daniel's hips and pressed their bodies together, claiming his mouth in a heated kiss. Their tongues tangled as Oliver's hands roamed, pulling Daniel's jeans lower until his cock sprang free, thick and heavy.

"**You're so fucking hot,**" Oliver murmured against Daniel's lips, his fingers trailing through the coarse hair and gripping his shaft firmly.

Daniel groaned, thrusting into Oliver's hand as the scent of musk and leather filled the air.

"**Do you always get this hard in the library?**" Oliver teased, stroking him slowly.

"**Only when someone like you is watching,**" Daniel shot back, his voice rough with need.

Oliver dropped to his knees, his lips brushing against Daniel's exposed cock.

"**Keep quiet,**" Oliver warned. "**Unless you want the entire library to hear how much you need this.**"

Daniel's fingers tangled in Oliver's hair as his mouth enveloped him, hot and wet.

. . .

Claiming the Moment

Oliver worked him expertly, his tongue teasing the sensitive slit before taking him deeper. Daniel struggled to keep still, his hips bucking against Oliver's mouth as books loomed silently around them.

"Fuck, Oliver," Daniel hissed, his voice barely above a whisper. **"You're gonna make me come."**

Oliver pulled back with a smirk. **"Not yet,"** he said, wiping his lips. **"You're not coming until I'm inside you."**

Daniel's eyes widened, his breath quickening.

"Right here?"

"Right here," Oliver growled, pulling him to his feet and leading him toward the back of the stacks, where shadows stretched long and dark.

Oliver pressed Daniel against a tall bookshelf, his hands roaming down his back, over his ass, and spreading him open.

"You need this, don't you?" Oliver whispered, grinding his cock against Daniel's bare skin.

"Yes," Daniel gasped. **"Please. Don't make me wait."**

Oliver spat into his hand, slicking his cock before pressing the tip against Daniel's tight hole.

"Relax," Oliver ordered. **"Take me."**

He pushed in slowly, savoring the stretch as Daniel moaned into the crook of his arm.

"Fuck, you're tight," Oliver groaned, driving deeper until he was buried to the hilt. **"You feel incredible."**

Daniel's fingers clawed at the shelves, his body rocking with every thrust.

"Harder," Daniel begged.

Oliver obliged, pounding into him with raw, unrestrained hunger, the sound of skin slapping against skin mingling with the faint creak of the shelves.

"You like being fucked in the library?" Oliver growled.

"Yes! Don't stop!"

Coming Undone

Oliver reached around and gripped Daniel's cock, stroking him in time with his thrusts.

"Come for me," he demanded.

Daniel's body seized, and he cried out as he came, spilling hot streams of cum onto the floor. The sight sent Oliver over the edge, and with one final thrust, he buried himself deep, filling Daniel with thick pulses of cum.

They stayed like that for a moment, panting and spent, before Oliver pulled out and turned Daniel to face him.

"You're fucking mine now," Oliver said, biting Daniel's lip.

"And you're not getting rid of me," Daniel shot back with a grin.

The Secret Connection

The following day, Daniel returned to the library. His legs ached, and his lips still tingled from Oliver's kisses, but he couldn't stay away.

He found Oliver at their usual table, already deep in a manuscript.

"We need to stop meeting like this," Daniel teased, sliding into the seat across from him.

Oliver smirked. **"Or maybe we need to start meeting like this more often."**

Daniel's cock stirred at the thought, and he knew this was only the beginning.

8
LOVE IN THE LIBRARY

T he Invitation

In the main reading room of the Bodleian Library, Oliver's sharp eyes locked onto Daniel, who was seated at a table surrounded by stacks of Elizabethan literature. Their gazes met, a silent challenge sparking between them. Oliver tilted his head toward the shadowy maze of shelves in the far corner, signaling for Daniel to follow.

Without hesitation, Daniel rose, his broad shoulders and confident stride turning more than a few heads as he crossed the room. The promise of what was about to unfold hung thick in the air, making Oliver's pulse quicken.

SECRETS AMONG THE STACKS

They disappeared into the dimly lit labyrinth of bookshelves, their footsteps echoing softly on the polished floor. Hidden from prying eyes, their tension mounted.

"You've been teasing me all day," Oliver murmured, his voice low and rough as he stepped closer.

"I like watching you squirm," Daniel replied, his eyes flickering down to the bulge in Oliver's jeans.

Oliver smirked, closing the space between them. His hands were quick, unzipping Daniel's jeans and tugging them down. Daniel followed suit, and within moments, they stood in their tight briefs, the evidence of their arousal straining against the fabric.

Daniel gasped as Oliver's eyes raked over his body, pausing on the thick, pulsing outline in his briefs.

"Fuck, you're perfect," Oliver growled, reaching out to pull Daniel's underwear down and exposing his hard, dripping cock.

Daniel's breath hitched as Oliver dropped to his knees, his fingers tracing the length of his shaft.

"You've been thinking about this all day, haven't you?" Oliver teased, pressing his lips against the tip.

"Yes," Daniel moaned, his hips thrusting forward. **"Do it."**

Oliver didn't need further encouragement. He swallowed Daniel's cock hungrily, his tongue swirling around the head before taking him deeper, his throat tightening as Daniel's hands tangled in his hair.

Pinned Against the Shelves

The sound of books shifting as Daniel pressed back against the shelves only heightened the thrill.

"Quiet," Oliver whispered, pulling off with a wet pop. **"Unless you want someone to find us."**

Daniel grinned. **"Maybe I do."**

Oliver's eyes darkened as he stood, shoving Daniel harder against the shelves.

"Then let's give them a show."

He spun Daniel around, pressing his chest to the wood and spreading his legs. Oliver's hands roamed over Daniel's body, fingers digging into his ass before spreading him open.

"You're fucking perfect," Oliver muttered, spitting onto his fingers and pushing one inside.

"Fuck," Daniel hissed, his body shivering as Oliver worked him open. "More."

Oliver added a second finger, twisting and stretching as Daniel rocked back against him.

"You're so fucking tight," Oliver groaned. "I need to be inside you."

THE POINT OF NO RETURN

Oliver pushed Daniel's shoulders forward, forcing him to arch as he spit into his palm and slicked his cock.

"Don't hold back," Daniel growled. "Give it to me."

With one smooth thrust, Oliver buried himself deep, and Daniel cried out, biting his lip to stifle the sound.

"God, you feel amazing," Oliver moaned, gripping Daniel's hips and driving into him harder.

The sound of skin slapping filled the narrow aisle, the danger of discovery adding fuel to their fire.

"You like being fucked in a library?" Oliver taunted. "You like knowing someone could walk in and see you taking my cock?"

"Yes!" Daniel gasped, his fingers clutching the shelf for balance.

. . .

Release and Ruin

Oliver reached around and wrapped his hand around Daniel's cock, stroking it in rhythm with his thrusts.

"Come for me," Oliver growled. **"Come while I'm buried inside you."**

Daniel's entire body tensed, and with a muffled cry, he exploded, thick ropes of cum splattering against the shelf and books.

The sight of Daniel falling apart pushed Oliver over the edge. With a final thrust, he groaned, filling Daniel with hot spurts of cum before collapsing against him.

They stood there for a moment, their bodies still trembling as they caught their breath.

"You're a fucking menace," Daniel said, grinning as he turned to face Oliver.

Oliver smirked, running a hand through Daniel's damp hair. **"And you love it."**

A Forbidden Connection

In the weeks that followed, the library became more than just a sanctuary for books and knowledge—it became their sanctuary. Hidden among the shelves, they explored each other's bodies and desires, pushing boundaries and daring discovery.

Each encounter left them hungrier for more, their bond growing deeper with every whispered word and a stolen kiss. But the thrill of their forbidden connection only added fuel to the fire, making it impossible to stop.

"You coming back tomorrow?" Daniel asked one evening, brushing his lips against Oliver's.

"Always," Oliver replied, his hand slipping into Daniel's waistband.

And as they disappeared once more into the shadows, they knew this was only the beginning of something raw, dangerous, and unforgettable.

Hot Public Sex

As they continued to explore one another with their hands and mouths, Oliver felt a sense of completion that went beyond mere physical pleasure. It was as if they were two halves of a whole, each completing the other in ways that neither could have imagined possible. Both men were pleased to see three other young students watching them from the end of the rank of books. All were busily rubbing their hands on their cocks. This was exactly what Daniel and Oliver hoped for—hot public sex.

As they stood there, lost in each other's embrace, they knew this was something special that would change them both forever. As their passion reached its peak, Oliver suddenly pulled away from Daniel, leaving him gasping for breath and desperate for release. "Not yet," he whispered hoarsely, standing up abruptly and pulling Daniel to his feet. **I have something else in mind**."

Oliver's descent to the cool marble was swift and silent; his eyes locked on Daniel with a predatory yet playful intensity. With practiced ease, he took Daniel's impressive length into his mouth, his lips wrapping around it with an enthusiasm that left no room for hesitation.

Climax

The initial challenge of accommodating such girth was formidable, indeed, but Oliver was undeterred. The rapturous moans and fervent whispers of approval from the students watching only fuelled his drive further.

The experience of taking the virile man's hot cock deep into his throat was an intoxicating blend of pleasure and power, a sensation made all the more potent by the hungry eyes upon them. It was as though they had become the stars of their illicit show, with Oliver relishing the role of a passionate celebrity basking under the unwavering spotlight of their audience's attention.

As moments passed, Daniel surrendered to the enthusiasm, thrusting with unrestrained vigor as he delivered his heated essence straight into Oliver's waiting mouth. Concurrently, Oliver reached his zenith, spilling his release onto the polished stone.

From the trio of onlookers, a chorus of profound exhalations filled the air as they, too, found their climax, their jeans visibly strained by the evidence of their ejaculations. The tableau before them was undeniably charged with eroticism.

In the Shadows

As the calendar pages fell like autumn leaves, marking the passage of time, Daniel and Oliver's bond deepened. Once confined to the intellectual, their dialogues became personal as they entrusted each other with their innermost musings and emotions.

Seated shoulder to shoulder among the antiquated tomes that whispered tales of yesteryear, they understood they had stumbled upon a rare treasure in each other's company.

This burgeoning relationship, however, was tinged with the bittersweet realization that it was doomed to exist only within the shadows of their clandestine meetings. In the hallowed corridors where echoes of the past mingled with the present, their union was a forbidden dance, enticing in its taboo.

Despite the risks that loomed over them like storm clouds, the magnetic pull between them was as undeniable and powerful as the gravitational force that bound the Earth to the sun.

9

FORBIDDEN FLAME IGNITES

Obsessive Fantasies

Daniel lay sprawled across his bed, his mind churning with vivid images of Oliver—naked, bound, and begging. The hunger in Oliver's eyes during their last encounter had ignited something primal in Daniel: a need to claim and dominate and push boundaries until there was nothing left but surrender.

"You want it, don't you?" Oliver's voice echoed in Daniel's imagination, teasing and breathless.

Daniel's cock throbbed as he replayed the memory of Oliver's body writhing beneath his touch, yielding so easily to his control. He imagined Oliver tied to the bed, wrists bound in leather; his legs spread wide and vulnerable, ready to be taken.

His fingers slipped beneath the waistband of his boxers, curling around his aching shaft. The strokes began slow, deliberate, matching the rhythm of the scene building in his mind.

"You're mine tonight," Daniel whispered aloud, his voice thick with need.

Oliver's phantom moans filled the silence, growing louder as Daniel tightened his grip, his strokes quickening. He pictured Oliver's lips stretched wide, his tongue flicking across the head of Daniel's cock, teasing until Daniel snapped and fucked his mouth raw.

"Take it. Take every inch," Daniel growled, his hips lifting off the mattress as his orgasm surged.

Warmth spilled over his fingers, his body shuddering as the final echoes of pleasure washed through him. But the satisfaction was fleeting, replaced almost instantly by frustration. He needed more than fantasies—he needed Oliver, in the flesh, bound and begging beneath him.

Temptation in the Library

Later that afternoon, Daniel's pulse quickened as he slipped through the ancient stone corridors of the Radcliffe Camera. The library hummed with whispers and footsteps, but Daniel barely noticed. His focus was fixed on the forbidden meeting ahead.

Max Hornsby—his literature tutor, his secret obsession—was waiting. A former rugby player with broad shoulders and thighs carved from granite, Max exuded authority and raw masculinity. Daniel had spent months hungering for him, and now, the moment had arrived.

The narrow stairwell pressed in around him, the scent of old books mingling with anticipation. Every step closer to the hidden alcove felt like peeling away another layer of restraint.

"Close the door behind you," Max ordered the moment Daniel entered the secluded study room.

The door clicked shut, sealing them in a space where rules didn't apply.

"You've been distracting me," Max continued, leaning back in his chair, legs spread just enough to make Daniel's mouth water. **"I think it's time we settled this."**

Daniel's knees hit the floor without hesitation.

Max's belt was the first to go, the leather hissing as it slid free. He looped it around Daniel's wrists, binding them tightly behind his back.

"Look at you," Max murmured, his voice heavy with approval. **"So fucking eager to obey."**

Daniel's heart pounded as Max unzipped, freeing his thick, heavy cock. It bobbed temptingly close to Daniel's lips, the scent of pre-cum making his mouth water.

"Open," Max commanded, gripping Daniel's hair.

Daniel obeyed, letting Max push deep, the stretch forcing his throat to relax. He gagged briefly, but Max didn't ease up. Instead, he fucked Daniel's mouth in slow, deliberate thrusts, his grip tightening with every gasp and moan.

"You're mine," Max growled, his voice rough as he claimed Daniel's throat. **"And I'm going to ruin you."**

Daniel's cock strained against his jeans, desperate for friction, but the bindings held firm. The helplessness only made him harder.

"You love this, don't you?" Max taunted. **"Being used. Being owned."**

Daniel could only moan in response, his body trembling as Max drove deeper, using him until his rhythm broke.

With a sharp grunt, Max came hard, flooding Daniel's mouth. Daniel swallowed greedily, licking him clean before Max finally pulled away.

"**Good boy,**" Max murmured, untying the belt and running a hand through Daniel's hair. "**Now get up. We're not done.**"

Electric Anticipation

Daniel paused outside the Radcliffe Camera, his breath hitching as his professor's piercing gaze locked onto him. Max Hornsby—rugged, commanding, and impossibly seductive—rose from the bench where he'd been waiting, his posture exuding control.

The air between them pulsed with unspoken hunger, and as Daniel stepped closer, the tension coiled tighter.

"**You kept me waiting,**" Max murmured, his voice low and deliberate, each word igniting Daniel's nerves.

Daniel's hand shot out, gripping Max's tie and yanking him forward. Their mouths collided, raw and desperate, weeks of tension exploding in the heat of their kiss. Tongues tangled as Daniel pressed closer, his fingers tangling in Max's hair while Max's strong hands gripped Daniel's hips, pulling him flush against his firm body.

"**I can't wait any longer,**" Daniel growled, lips grazing Max's ear. "**Let's go.**"

Guiding Max toward a shaded bench beneath an ancient oak, Daniel sat down and pulled Max into his lap, their bodies aligning perfectly. The professor's broad chest heaved, his pupils dark with need.

"**You sure about this?**" Max asked, his voice a delicious rasp.

"**I've never been more sure.**"

Daniel's hands roamed over Max's torso, slipping beneath his shirt to explore taut muscles. Their lips met again, slower this time, savoring the taste and heat. As Daniel teased a nipple between his fingers, Max groaned, arching into the touch.

"You're a tease," Max panted.

"I'm just getting started."

An Audience Appears

A sudden shift in the atmosphere made Daniel glance up. Across the walkway, three men leaned against a railing, their eyes locked on the unfolding scene.

"We've got company," Max whispered, lips curling into a smirk. **"Enjoying the show, boys?"**

Daniel's pulse quickened, but instead of pulling away, he felt emboldened.

"Let them watch."

He pushed Max back against the bench, sliding a hand down to cup the hard bulge straining against Max's trousers. The professor's sharp intake of breath only fueled Daniel's confidence.

"You like being on display," Daniel teased, unfastening Max's belt and pulling it free with a hiss. **"Let's give them something to remember."**

Daniel shoved Max's trousers down to his knees, exposing the firm, sculpted curves of his ass. The men watching shifted, their breathing audible even from across the walkway.

"On your knees," Daniel ordered, his voice dropping into a commanding growl.

Max obeyed without hesitation, bracing himself against the bench as Daniel knelt behind him. Daniel spread him open, his tongue flicking out to taste, dragging wet heat across sensitive flesh. Max shuddered, moaning loudly enough to draw the watchers even closer.

"You're filthy," Daniel muttered between licks. **"And I fucking love it."**

Max pushed back against Daniel's face, silently begging for more. Daniel obliged, his tongue circling and pressing until Max was trembling.

"Please," Max gasped. **"I need you inside me."**

Daniel pulled away just long enough to shed his jeans, freeing his thick, pulsing cock.

"You ready for this?"

Max groaned and spread wider.

"Do it."

Raw Surrender

Daniel lined himself up, pressing the slick head of his cock against Max's entrance. He pushed slowly at first, savoring the stretch as Max's body yielded to him.

"You're so fucking tight," Daniel hissed, driving deeper.

Max gasped, his knuckles white as he gripped the bench. Daniel's thrusts grew harder, his hips snapping forward, driving Max closer to the edge.

"You like being fucked where anyone can see," Daniel taunted. **"You're such a dirty professor."**

"Yes—God, yes," Max panted, pushing back to meet each thrust.

The men watching stroked themselves openly now, groaning as

the scene unfolded. Daniel reached around to grip Max's cock, pumping in rhythm with his thrusts.

"Come for me," Daniel demanded.

Max cried out, his release spilling over Daniel's hand as his body clenched tight around Daniel's cock. The added pressure sent Daniel over the edge, burying himself deep as he came hard, his groans echoing through the shaded space.

They collapsed together, breaths ragged and bodies slick with sweat.

"We should probably move before someone calls security," Max said with a lazy grin.

Daniel smirked, tucking himself back into his jeans.

"Not until you're ready for round two."

Max's eyes darkened, promising more to come.

UNLEASHED DESIRE

Daniel's body surged forward, his thrusts hard and relentless, driving into his professor with precision and hunger. The sharp slap of flesh against flesh filled the room, mingling with Max's raw, unrestrained moans.

"Don't stop—God, don't stop!" Max pleaded, his voice hoarse with desperation.

Daniel gripped Max's hips tighter, holding him in place as he pounded deeper, pushing them both closer to the brink.

"You love this," Daniel growled, leaning down to bite the curve of Max's shoulder. **"Being used. Being fucked where anyone can see."**

Max's trembling legs betrayed his surrender, his body opening further to Daniel's demanding rhythm. Sweat glistened on their skin, the heat between them unbearable and intoxicating.

"More," Max begged. **"Harder."**

Daniel obliged, his movements turning feral, each thrust driving them both closer to collapse. The onlookers, still fixated on the illicit display, mirrored the urgency of the moment, stroking themselves as their eyes devoured every detail.

EXHIBITION OF LUST

The men surrounding them were no longer just observers—they were participants. Their hands moved in time with Daniel's thrusts, matching the rising tempo as if caught in a spell of shared lust.

"Look at them," Daniel whispered, tightening his grip on Max's hair and forcing him to meet the eyes of their audience. **"They're getting off to you."**

Max moaned louder, his body trembling under Daniel's control.

"They wish they could have you," Daniel taunted, his voice dripping with dominance. **"But you're mine."**

The chorus of heavy breathing and muffled groans surrounded them, adding fuel to their fire. Daniel's strokes became sharper, more erratic, as Max's cries of pleasure tipped into desperation.

"I'm going to come," Max gasped.

"Do it," Daniel ordered, his voice commanding. **"Let them see what I do to you."**

Max's release hit first, spilling over Daniel's hand as his entire body convulsed. The sight and sensation sent Daniel spiraling, his own climax tearing through him as he drove deep one final time, filling Max completely.

The audience followed suit, groaning as they reached their peaks, their sticky releases marking the space like a tribute to the raw display they had witnessed.

AFTERMATH OF ECSTASY

Panting and drenched in sweat, Daniel pulled out slowly, brushing a kiss along Max's shoulder as he collapsed against him. Their bodies remained entangled, unwilling to separate as the weight of what had just transpired settled over them.

"You're incredible," Daniel whispered, his lips brushing Max's ear.

Max turned, his eyes shining. **"So are you."**

But even as their breaths slowed, the moment lingered, sharp and alive. Daniel helped Max dress, his touch lingering longer than necessary, unwilling to let go.

Later, as Max walked away across the campus, Daniel hesitated, the professor's scent still clinging to his skin. The ache in his chest matched the fading heat between his legs.

Without thinking, Daniel sprinted after him, grabbing Max's arm just as the older man turned. Tears glistened in Max's eyes, and Daniel's heart tightened.

"Don't leave," Daniel said, his voice trembling. **"I can't let this end here. We need to figure this out—together."**

Max exhaled shakily, his lips parting, but no words came.

"Please," Daniel whispered, cupping Max's face in his hands. **"I think this could be something real."**

A tear rolled down Max's cheek as he nodded, his defenses crumbling. Without hesitation, Daniel drew him into a deep, lingering kiss.

The world fell away as they clung to each other, their passion igniting once more—not just as a release of lust, but as a promise of something deeper.

SECRETS IN THE SHADOWS

Daniel and Oliver slipped through the library like predators stalking prey, their movements deliberate and silent. The creak of the ancient wooden floor seemed amplified in the dim, cavernous space, each step driving their pulses higher.

The scent of aged paper and polished wood clung to the air—a mixture of history and secrecy that heightened their senses. Shelves loomed like sentinels, shielding them from prying eyes as they pressed deeper into the labyrinth of books and shadows.

"No one comes back here this late," Oliver whispered, his voice low and rough, already thick with anticipation.

"Good," Daniel replied, his hand brushing Oliver's hip as they turned down a narrow aisle. **"Because I don't want to hold back tonight."**

They found it—a dark, narrow alcove tucked behind towering shelves, isolated and perfect. Daniel's heart hammered as he pulled Oliver inside, the small space closing around them like a secret chamber.

"We shouldn't," Oliver murmured, but the hunger in his eyes betrayed him.

"We're going to." Daniel shoved Oliver against the wall, pinning him with his body. Their mouths collided, tongues tangling in a kiss that was more hunger than finesse.

Hands roamed freely—Daniel's fingers tracing the ridges of Oliver's torso, Oliver's nails dragging down Daniel's back. The darkness made every touch feel illicit, magnified by the muffled sound of pages turning somewhere in the distance.

"Keep quiet," Daniel warned, his lips brushing against Oliver's jaw. **"Unless you want the whole library to hear how badly you need this."**

Bound in Desire

Daniel yanked off Oliver's belt with a sharp hiss, looping it around his wrists and tightening it behind his back.

"What are you doing?" Oliver's voice trembled, but his cock strained hard against his jeans, betraying his arousal.

"Making sure you behave," Daniel growled, stepping back to admire his handiwork. **"Now, stay still."**

He dropped to his knees, unzipping Oliver's jeans and pulling them down just enough to expose his hardness.

"Fuck," Oliver hissed as Daniel's tongue flicked out, tasting him.

Daniel's lips wrapped around the head, sucking slowly, deliberately teasing. Oliver squirmed, but the belt held him in place.

"You're not going anywhere," Daniel said, pulling off with a wicked grin. **"I'll take my time with you."**

Oliver's moans grew louder as Daniel worked him over, licking, sucking, and teasing until his legs trembled. But Daniel wasn't finished.

He spun Oliver around, forcing him to brace against the wall. With one sharp tug, he yanked Oliver's jeans lower, exposing the firm curves of his ass.

"**You've been thinking about this all day, haven't you?**" Daniel whispered, kneeling behind him. "**Walking around with this tight little ass, knowing it belongs to me.**"

Oliver whimpered as Daniel's tongue pressed between his cheeks, teasing the sensitive ring of muscle. His hips bucked, but Daniel held him steady, devouring him until Oliver's pleas dissolved into incoherent moans.

"**Tell me what you want,**" Daniel demanded, his breath hot against Oliver's skin.

"**I want you inside me—now,**" Oliver begged.

Taking Control

Daniel stood, pushing his jeans down and pressing his cock against Oliver's entrance.

"**Beg me,**" Daniel commanded, his voice low and dangerous.

"**Please,**" Oliver gasped. "**Fuck me—make me yours.**"

Daniel pushed in slowly, inch by inch, savoring the way Oliver's body opened for him.

"**You're so tight,**" Daniel growled, gripping Oliver's hips as he drove deeper. "**You love being used like this, don't you?**"

Oliver's only response was a desperate moan as Daniel began to move, thrusting harder, faster. The belt binding Oliver's wrists kept him helpless, pinned against the wall as Daniel claimed him.

"**You look so fucking good like this,**" Daniel said between thrusts. "**Bent over, begging for more.**"

The rhythm is built, with each stroke pushing Oliver closer to the edge.

Daniel reached around, gripping Oliver's cock and stroking in time with his thrusts. The tension in Oliver's body snapped first, his climax hitting with violent intensity.

"Fuck—Daniel!" Oliver cried out, his release coating the wall as his body shuddered.

Daniel didn't stop, riding the aftershocks until his own orgasm overtook him, spilling deep inside Oliver with a guttural groan.

They collapsed against the wall, panting, the air thick with sweat and the scent of sex.

Aftermath in the Shadows

Untying the belt, Daniel turned Oliver around, pulling him into a slow, lazy kiss.

"You're dangerous," Oliver said, his lips curving into a grin.

"You love it," Daniel replied, tucking Oliver's cock back into his jeans.

They dressed in silence, their movements unhurried, savoring the heat that lingered between them. As they slipped out of the alcove, Daniel caught Oliver's hand, lacing their fingers together.

"This isn't over," Daniel said.

Oliver squeezed his hand, a mischievous gleam in his eyes. **"Not even close."**

Confessions in the Dark

Daniel and Oliver lay tangled together, their slick bodies pressed so tightly that it was impossible to tell where one ended and the other began. The air between them hung heavy with heat and the fading echoes of their moans. Daniel traced slow, deliberate circles across Oliver's chest, his fingers lingering over sensitive spots that made Oliver shiver.

"You know," Daniel began, his voice low and breathless, **"I've never felt this way before—with anyone."**

Oliver stirred, his eyes half-lidded as he looked up at Daniel. **"You're serious?"**

"Dead serious." Daniel's fingers trailed down Oliver's stomach, teasing the waistband of his briefs. **"I think I might like Max. Really like him."**

Oliver smirked, his lips curving into something wicked. **"Your professor? You kinky bastard."**

Daniel leaned in, brushing his mouth against Oliver's. **"You love it. Admit it."**

"Maybe I do," Oliver murmured, biting Daniel's lower lip. **"But right now, I want you to stop talking about him and show me just how horny you really are."**

Daniel wasted no time, pushing Oliver onto his back and pinning his wrists above his head. The shift in control made Oliver moan softly, his breath catching as Daniel kissed his way down his chest.

"You're so fucking hot like this," Daniel growled, his teeth grazing a nipple before sucking it hard enough to leave a mark.

Oliver arched beneath him, his hips grinding upward. **"Don't stop,"** he begged, his voice a breathy plea.

Daniel trailed lower, his tongue leaving wet streaks down Oliver's stomach until he reached the waistband of his jeans. With practiced ease, he unbuttoned and unzipped, yanking them down to reveal Oliver's cock, thick and already leaking.

"Damn, you're hard for me," Daniel said, his voice husky.

Oliver groaned as Daniel's fingers wrapped around him, stroking with firm, deliberate movements.

"You like this?" Daniel taunted, flicking his tongue across the tip.

"Yes," Oliver gasped. **"Fuck, yes."**

Daniel didn't wait—he took Oliver deep, swallowing him inch by inch. The heat of his mouth made Oliver writhe, his fingers gripping Daniel's hair and holding tight as Daniel set a punishing rhythm.

"You're not going to last," Daniel teased, pulling back just enough to speak before plunging down again.

Boundaries Broken

Daniel released Oliver's cock with a wet pop and flipped him onto his stomach, pulling his hips up. He shoved Oliver's jeans further down, exposing his perfect ass.

"Spread your legs for me," Daniel commanded.

Oliver obeyed without hesitation, his breath hitching as Daniel's hands gripped his cheeks, spreading them wide.

"Look at you," Daniel whispered, dragging his tongue slowly over the sensitive skin. **"So desperate to be fucked."**

Oliver whimpered as Daniel's tongue circled and pressed against his tight entrance, slicking him open.

"Please," Oliver begged, pushing back against Daniel's face.

Daniel pulled away, unzipping his jeans and stroking himself as he lined up.

"You ready?"

"God, yes—fuck me."

Daniel pressed forward, the stretch making Oliver moan as he sank in slowly, inch by inch.

"So fucking tight," Daniel groaned, his grip tightening on Oliver's hips.

Oliver pushed back, taking him deeper. "Harder. Don't hold back."

Daniel's rhythm grew brutal, his hips slamming into Oliver as their bodies collided. The sound of skin on skin echoed in the dim space, accompanied by Oliver's cries and Daniel's guttural groans.

EXHIBITION IN THE LIBRARY

As Daniel fucked Oliver, the thought of their location heightened the thrill. Ancient books surrounded them, silent witnesses to their raw, unrestrained passion.

"Anyone could walk in and see you like this," Daniel growled, leaning down to bite Oliver's shoulder. "Bent over, dripping for me."

Oliver moaned louder, his cock leaking onto the wooden floor beneath them.

"You love being my dirty little secret, don't you?"

"Yes," Oliver gasped, his voice trembling.

Daniel reached around, stroking Oliver's cock in time with his thrusts.

"Come for me," Daniel demanded.

Oliver cried out, his body shaking as he climaxed, spilling over Daniel's hand. The tight clench of his orgasm pushed Daniel over the edge, and he drove deep one last time, filling Oliver with a groan.

Aftermath Among the Books

They collapsed in a heap, their breath heavy and mingling as they came down from the high. Daniel pressed a kiss to Oliver's shoulder, his fingers still tracing patterns over sweat-damp skin.

"We're going to get caught one of these days," Oliver muttered, but there was no fear in his voice—only satisfaction.

"Then we'll give them a show," Daniel replied, smirking as he pulled Oliver into another kiss.

As they dressed, the library seemed to exhale around them, absorbing the echoes of their passion into its ancient walls. Their footsteps faded, leaving behind only the scent of sweat and sex, and the unspoken promise of another rendezvous.

In the hallowed silence of the Radcliffe Camera, Daniel and Oliver's gasps and moans shattered the stillness, a forbidden melody that danced off marble and stone. The domed ceiling seemed to cradle their cries, folding them into the centuries-old fabric of secrets and confessions that lingered within its walls.

"You feel so fucking good," Daniel growled, his voice echoing softly as he pinned Oliver against the cold stone. **"I can't get enough of you."**

Oliver arched beneath him, his fingers clutching at Daniel's back. **"Then don't stop,"** he whispered, the command breathless and raw.

They moved together, hips colliding with an urgency that matched the fire burning between them. Their hunger was primal and unapologetic—a hunger no amount of secrecy could suppress.

. . .

The Library's Collusion

Books lined the shelves, silent witnesses to their indiscretions, yet the room itself seemed to conspire with them, absorbing every thrust, every desperate gasp, as though protecting their passion.

Daniel reached down, gripping Oliver's wrists and forcing them above his head.

"You're mine here," Daniel murmured, his breath hot against Oliver's neck. **"Right here, where anyone could find us."**

Oliver shivered, his cock throbbing as Daniel's words dripped with dominance.

"Then claim me," Oliver moaned.

Daniel pressed deeper, their bodies grinding against the unforgiving stone. The contrast of heat and cold heightened every sensation.

"I already have," Daniel said, his voice thick with lust as he thrust harder, pushing Oliver closer to the edge.

Ritual of Desire

They fucked with reckless abandon, their rhythm matching the steady thud of history echoing beneath their feet. Oliver's moans filled the space, rising and falling like a sacred chant.

"Quiet," Daniel hissed, his hand sliding over Oliver's mouth. **"Or do you want someone to catch us?"**

Oliver groaned against Daniel's palm, his muffled cries vibrating through the air. The thrill of being overheard only fueled their urgency, their bodies slick and trembling as they edged closer to release.

Daniel let go of Oliver's mouth just long enough to spit into his palm and stroke him hard and fast.

"Come for me," Daniel demanded.

Oliver's body tensed, and with a strangled moan, he spilled over Daniel's fingers. The heat and tightness of his climax sent Daniel spiraling after him, his cock pulsing as he emptied himself deep inside Oliver.

Panting, they leaned against the wall; their bodies still joined as they came down from the high. Daniel brushed sweat-soaked hair from Oliver's forehead, placing a lingering kiss against his temple.

"Think the books will keep our secret?" Oliver asked, his voice shaky but teasing.

Daniel smirked. **"They better. Otherwise, we'll have to come back and make sure."**

Pulling up their clothes, they straightened themselves, but the evidence of their passion lingered—the scent of sweat and sex clinging to the air, their marks on each other's skin a reminder of what had just passed.

As they slipped back into the shadows, leaving the library behind, Daniel glanced back at the shelves—silent, ancient, and complicit. The Radcliffe Camera had witnessed their desires and held their secrets, just as it had done for countless others before them.

Though they stepped into the world beyond the library's walls, their connection—carved into the stone and etched into the air—remained, preserved by the library's timeless embrace.

10
SANCTUARY'S SECRETS

A Tense Invitation

The sun dipped below the horizon as Daniel approached Dr. Max Hornsby's faculty office, his pulse quickening with every step. The hot young professor's invitation for a "late-afternoon study session" had sounded professional on paper. Still, Daniel couldn't ignore the heat that lingered from their last encounter outside the Radcliffe Camera.

Excitement churned in his stomach, tangled with nerves. The casual hookup had spiraled into something far more intense than either of them had planned. Max's vulnerability and the unexpected emotional connection they'd shared had left Daniel unsteady—and desperate for more.

CROSSING THE THRESHOLD

Max stood behind his desk when Daniel entered, looking at every bit of the fantasy Daniel couldn't shake. The professor's chiseled jaw and piercing eyes commanded attention, but it was the barely concealed bulge in his tailored trousers that made Daniel's mouth go dry.

"Daniel," Max said, his voice warm but hesitant. **"I'm so glad you came. We have a lot of material to cover tonight."**

Daniel couldn't ignore the flicker of tension in Max's expression as he stepped closer.

"Before we begin," Max continued, **"I need to apologize for what happened outside the Radcliffe Camera. It was inappropriate. I crossed a line, and I hope you can forgive me."**

Daniel's heart twisted at the sincerity in Max's voice—and the single tear that slipped down his cheek. Without thinking, Daniel closed the distance between them, pulling Max into a firm embrace.

"You don't need to apologize," Daniel whispered. **"You see me as a student, but I'm 21. I'm not a kid. In two weeks, I'll graduate. I won't be your student anymore."**

Max pulled back just enough to meet Daniel's gaze, his lips trembling. **"Are you really sure about this? About us?"**

"As sure as I've ever been," Daniel said, brushing Max's tear away with his thumb. **"I've never felt this way about anyone before. It scares me too—but I want to find out where this can go."**

Daniel took a seat across from Max, struggling to keep things professional even as the air between them thickened with tension.

"So," Max began, leaning back in his chair and letting his gaze linger, **"what do you like to do for fun, Daniel?"**

Daniel hesitated, then smirked. **"Fun? Who has time for that?"** He let the moment hang before adding, **"I like dancing in clubs sometimes."**

Max's eyes darkened. **"I used to be quite the dancer myself back in college,"** he said, his tone dripping with suggestion. **"But my tastes in dance partners have... evolved."**

Max's wink sent a jolt of heat straight to Daniel's core.

"And what about hobbies?" Max pressed. **"Anything else you enjoy?"**

Daniel swallowed hard. **"Early morning runs. Just me, the sunrise, and a pair of running shorts."**

Max's jaw tightened. His eyes roamed over Daniel's body, clearly picturing him in nothing but tight nylon shorts—and Daniel knew it.

"Is that all?" Max asked, his voice rough.

"I like to cook," Daniel added, but the glint in Max's eyes told him they were no longer talking about food.

From Words to Action

Max stood, rounding the desk and leaning against it just inches from Daniel.

"Cooking, huh?" Max's voice dropped. **"Maybe you can show me what else you're good at."**

Daniel rose slowly, closing the gap.

"I think you already know what I'm good at," Daniel murmured, his fingers trailing along Max's tie before tugging him down into a searing kiss.

Max responded instantly, his hands gripping Daniel's waist and pulling him close.

"Lock the door," Max growled.

Daniel obeyed, but Max was already unbuttoning his shirt, exposing smooth, toned skin.

"You've been teasing me all night," Max said, pushing Daniel onto the desk. **"Now it's my turn."**

Max yanked Daniel's jeans down, leaving him bare except for his briefs, the thin fabric doing nothing to hide his arousal.

"Fuck," Max breathed, running his hand over Daniel's bulge before pulling the briefs down and freeing him.

Daniel's cock throbbed, hard and ready, as Max dropped to his knees.

"I've wanted this since the first time I saw you," Max confessed before taking Daniel into his mouth.

Daniel groaned, his fingers tangling in Max's hair as the professor sucked him deep, setting a slow, torturous rhythm.

"Don't stop," Daniel begged.

Max didn't—he hollowed his cheeks and worked Daniel over until he was trembling, teetering on the edge. But just as Daniel was about to come, Max pulled back.

"Not yet," Max said, standing and spinning Daniel around to bend him over the desk.

DESKS AND DISCIPLINE

Max spit into his palm, slicking himself before pressing the head of his cock against Daniel's entrance.

"You need to learn patience," Max growled, pushing in slowly.

Daniel gasped, his hands gripping the desk as Max filled him inch by inch.

"**You feel so fucking good,**" Max groaned, his hands gripping Daniel's hips as he began to move.

The sound of their bodies colliding filled the office, mingling with Daniel's moans and Max's curses.

"**Harder,**" Daniel demanded, pushing back against Max's thrusts.

Max obliged, pounding into him until the desk shook beneath them.

"**Come for me,**" Max ordered, reaching around to stroke Daniel's cock.

Daniel cried out, his orgasm tearing through him as Max followed, spilling deep inside him.

A Deepening Connection

As the afternoon sun filtered through the windows, casting warm streaks of light across the room, Daniel and Max's conversation shifted from casual banter to confessions. Favorite books gave way to childhood fears, and guilty pleasures turned into raw truths.

"**You make it so easy to talk to you,**" Daniel admitted, his voice low and sincere.

Max smiled, his gaze steady but tinged with vulnerability. "**I feel the same way. It's like we speak the same language.**"

Daniel's pulse quickened. Something was intoxicating about Max —not just his looks, but the way he listened, the way he made Daniel feel completely seen.

As the conversation slowed and Daniel began to gather his things, Max stopped him with a single sentence.

"**Daniel, I hope you enjoyed spending time with me as much as I did with you.**"

Daniel froze, the heat building between them, reigniting instantly.

"I definitely did," Daniel said, his voice barely more than a whisper.

They stood there, tension crackling in the air until Max closed the distance. Without another word, their lips collided, the kiss raw and urgent. Hands tore at buttons and belts, shedding layers until their toned, eager bodies were exposed.

Max's lips trailed down Daniel's neck, biting and sucking as Daniel groaned, pulling Max closer.

"You've been teasing me all day," Max growled, shoving Daniel onto the desk. **"Now I'm going to make you beg."**

"I don't beg," Daniel shot back, but his cock was already rock-hard, betraying his need.

Max smirked. **"You will."**

Descent into Desire

Max dropped to his knees, his eyes locked on Daniel's as he took Daniel's cock into his mouth, slow and deliberate.

"Fuck," Daniel moaned, threading his fingers through Max's hair and guiding his movements.

Max's tongue worked expertly, swirling around the head before taking him deeper, hollowing his cheeks and sucking with hungry precision.

"You're so fucking good at that," Daniel gasped, his hips bucking forward.

But Max didn't let him finish. He pulled back just long enough to grin wickedly before pushing Daniel onto his stomach and spreading him wide.

"Don't move," Max commanded.

Daniel shivered as Max's tongue traced circles around his hole, teasing before pushing inside.

"Oh my God," Daniel groaned, his fists gripping the desk as Max worked him open with his tongue and fingers.

"You're ready," Max murmured, rising behind him and pressing the head of his cock against Daniel's entrance.

"Do it," Daniel demanded, looking back over his shoulder.

Max thrust forward, sinking in slowly, stretching Daniel until he moaned from the pressure.

Max gripped Daniel's hips, setting a brutal rhythm as he fucked him against the desk. The sharp slap of skin echoed in the room, mingling with Daniel's gasps and Max's grunts.

"You like being fucked like this, don't you?" Max growled, his voice thick with lust.

"Yes—God, yes!" Daniel cried out, pushing back to meet every thrust.

Max leaned down, biting Daniel's shoulder as he reached around to stroke him.

"Come for me," Max ordered, his voice commanding.

Daniel's body tensed, and with a guttural moan, he came hard, spilling across the desk. Max followed moments later, driving deep and filling Daniel as his body shook with release.

THE AFTERGLOW

Spent and breathless, they collapsed onto the desk, their bodies slick with sweat and cum.

"**Holy shit,**" Daniel muttered, running a hand through his hair.

Max laughed, brushing his fingers down Daniel's spine. "**I'm not done with you yet.**"

"**You'll have to give me a minute,**" Daniel said, smirking.

As they cleaned up, Max leaned back against the desk, still catching his breath.

"**That was incredible,**" he said softly.

Daniel grinned, pulling on his shirt. "**Me neither.**" He paused before adding, "**You gonna cry again?**"

Max punched him playfully, but the lighthearted moment shifted when Max's expression softened.

"**Daniel, do you think you could ever love an older man?**" Max asked, his voice quieter now.

Daniel smirked. "**You're 32. That's hardly ancient. But if this is your way of asking me to call you 'Daddy,' I'm definitely open to it.**"

Max laughed, his cheeks flushing, but his eyes burned with something deeper.

"**I'm serious,**" he said.

Daniel stepped closer, cupping Max's face. "**So am I. Let's see where this goes.**"

New Beginnings

Max kissed him again, slower this time, as if savoring the moment.

"**We're just getting started,**" Max murmured.

Daniel nodded, his pulse quickening all over again.

They'd explored their bodies and tested their limits, but as the sun dipped below the horizon, both men knew the real journey—the one that mixed lust with something dangerously close to love—was only beginning.

Obedience and Devotion

Daniel lay sprawled across Max's desk; his head tilted back as Max straddled his face, presenting his ass like an offering. The older man groaned, gripping the edge of the desk for balance as Daniel's tongue explored his tight, musky hole.

"Fuck, Daniel," Max moaned, rocking his hips and grinding down. **"You know exactly how I like it."**

Daniel growled in response, spreading Max wider and burying his face deeper. His tongue flicked, probed, and circled, driving Max wild with every wet, deliberate motion.

"Don't stop," Max ordered, his voice raw and demanding.

Daniel's hands gripped Max's firm cheeks, pulling him down harder as his tongue slid deeper, tasting him, owning him. The room filled with the sounds of slick, wet pleasure and Max's breathless moans, echoing off the office walls.

"You're going to make me lose it," Max gasped, looking down at Daniel with lust-darkened eyes.

Max leaned forward, pressing his hands flat against the desk to steady himself as Daniel's tongue pushed him closer to the edge.

"You're filthy," Max hissed, his body trembling. **"And I fucking love it."**

Daniel pulled back just long enough to smirk before diving in again, his lips latching onto Max's rim as if he couldn't get enough.

"You taste so good," Daniel murmured between licks.

Max's cock throbbed, leaking pre-cum onto Daniel's chest as he rode his face, surrendering completely.

"You're mine," Daniel growled. **"And when I'm done with you, you won't be able to walk out of this office."**

Max slid off Daniel's face, panting, and immediately flipped onto his back, spreading his legs wide.

"Take me," Max demanded, his voice hoarse. **"Now."**

Daniel didn't hesitate. He lined himself up, pressing the thick head of his cock against Max's slicked hole before pushing inside.

"Jesus, Max—you're so fucking tight," Daniel groaned, his hands digging into Max's thighs as he thrust deeper.

Max's nails raked down Daniel's back. **"Harder. Don't hold back."**

The rhythm built quickly, with hard, punishing thrusts that sent the desk creaking beneath them. The sound of skin slapping against skin filled the air, joined by their grunts and moans.

"You love getting fucked like this, don't you?" Daniel growled, gripping Max's legs and pushing them higher.

"Yes! God, yes!" Max cried out.

Sweat dripped from their bodies as Daniel pounded into Max, each thrust pushing them closer to the edge.

Explosive Release

Max's cock jerked between them, the pressure too much to bear.

"I'm coming—fuck—I'm coming!" Max shouted as his release exploded, coating both their stomachs in thick streams of cum.

The sight of Max's orgasm pushed Daniel over the edge. He pulled out just in time, stroking himself until his cum splattered across Max's chest and ass.

"Fuck," Daniel groaned, collapsing onto Max's spent body.

Max dragged Daniel into a kiss, messy and unrestrained, tasting sweat and lust.

"You're unbelievable," Max whispered. **"No one's ever made me feel this way."**

Their bodies tangled together as they caught their breath, their fingers tracing lazy patterns over slick skin.

"That was insane," Daniel said, grinning. **"I don't think I'll ever get enough of you."**

Max smirked, pulling Daniel closer. **"Good. Because I'm not done with you yet."**

They kissed again, slower this time—less frantic but no less intense. Daniel felt the shift between them, something deeper stirring beneath the surface.

"Do you think this could be more than just... this?" Max asked, his voice softer now.

Daniel leaned in, brushing his lips against Max's. **"I think it already is."**

Max's eyes shone with emotion as he pulled Daniel into another kiss, his body already stirring with renewed hunger.

Uncharted Territories

They didn't speak as Max rolled Daniel onto his back, pinning him to the desk and kissing down his chest.

"Round two?" Daniel teased, smirking.

"Round two," Max confirmed, spreading Daniel's legs and diving back in with renewed fervor.

As their bodies moved together again, it was clear this wasn't just about lust anymore. It was about surrender, trust, and an undeniable connection that both terrified and thrilled them.

They knew this was only the beginning—an exploration of passion, power, and vulnerability that would take them to places neither had dared to go before.

11
YOU ARE WHAT YOU READ

L iterary Seduction

Under the dim glow of the office lamp, their bodies still slick with sweat and the lingering scent of musk, Daniel, Max, and their two lovers sprawled among scattered books, their pages brimming with tales of passion, betrayal, and forbidden desires. The mingling aroma of sex and aged paper created an intoxicating haze, blurring the line between reality and fantasy.

Max leaned back against the desk, his shirt unbuttoned and his chest heaving, a mischievous glint in his eye as he thumbed through a worn volume of Shakespeare's sonnets.

"Daniel," Max purred, his voice low and seductive. What if we turned these words into something more? Something we can feel, taste, and touch?"

Daniel's lips curled into a wicked smile. **"You mean bring literature to life? Turn the passion in these pages into something real?"**

Max stepped closer, his eyes burning. **"Exactly. Imagine it—the** lust of Dorian Gray unchained, or the raw hunger of Achilles and Patroclus freed from myth."

Becoming the Characters

Daniel shivered as Max's words sank in, awakening his imagination. He picked up *The Picture of Dorian Gray* and held it out.

"Let's rewrite their stories," Daniel said, his voice thick with desire. "Give them the endings—or the beginnings—they were denied."

Max smirked, pulling Daniel close until their bodies aligned. "I'll be Heathcliff," Max growled. "Brooding, possessive, and utterly undone by desire."

Daniel leaned in, whispering, "Then I'll be Darcy—polished but desperate, craving your touch."

The tension in the room shifted, charged with anticipation, as the literary fantasies they had conjured began to materialize. Daniel's fingers trailed down Max's chest, undoing the remaining buttons as if stripping away layers of propriety.

"Shall I compare thee to a summer's day?" Daniel murmured, his lips brushing against Max's before claiming them in a searing kiss.

Max's hands gripped Daniel's waist, pulling him closer. "The only way to rid oneself of temptation," he whispered, his breath hot against Daniel's ear, "is to yield to it."

Their bodies pressed together, heat rising as they began their own sonnet—a symphony of tongues, teeth, and moans. Max guided Daniel backward, easing him onto the desk and pinning him down.

"You're mine," Max growled, trailing kisses down Daniel's neck. **"Just like Dorian was bound to his portrait—I'll make sure your body remembers this moment forever."**

Passion and Poetry

Max's hands explored Daniel's body as if he were tracing poetry into his flesh, his touch reverent yet insistent. Daniel gasped as Max's mouth found his nipples, teasing them into stiff peaks before continuing lower.

"I'll worship you," Max promised, spreading Daniel's legs and pressing his tongue against the tight entrance he'd been aching to taste.

Daniel moaned, his fingers gripping the edge of the desk as Max devoured him.

"Fuck, Max," Daniel gasped. **"Don't stop."**

Max's tongue flicked and pressed, pushing deeper, leaving Daniel squirming and breathless.

"I need you inside me," Daniel pleaded.

Max stood, unbuckling his belt and letting his trousers drop, his cock hard and dripping as he stroked it.

"Turn over," Max ordered, his voice sharp.

Daniel obeyed, pressing his chest against the desk as Max lined up behind him.

"You want this?" Max teased, rubbing the head of his cock against Daniel's hole.

"God, yes—fuck me," Daniel demanded.

Max thrust forward, filling Daniel inch by inch.

"So tight," Max groaned, gripping Daniel's hips and driving deeper. **"You feel fucking perfect."**

Epic Climaxes

The sound of flesh slapping against flesh echoed in the room, accompanied by grunts and gasps. Max's rhythm grew harder and faster, with each thrust pushing Daniel closer to the edge.

"You love this, don't you?" Max growled. **"Being bent over my desk like a dirty little slut."**

Daniel moaned in response, his cock dripping onto the polished wood.

"Come for me," Max commanded, reaching around to stroke Daniel's cock.

Daniel's body tensed, his orgasm tearing through him as he spilled onto the desk. Max followed moments later, his grip tightening as he filled Daniel with his release.

Collapsed against each other, their bodies slick with sweat and cum, Max leaned down and kissed Daniel's shoulder.

"We're not done," Max murmured.

Daniel smirked, still catching his breath. **"Good. Because I'm already ready for round two."**

They lay entangled, surrounded by open books and discarded clothes, their passion echoing the words that had inspired them.

"We've written our own story tonight," Max said softly, tracing lazy circles on Daniel's back.

Daniel grinned. **"And we're only on the first chapter."**

As the first light of dawn crept through the window, their bodies stirred again, eager to continue what they had begun.

The books would bear witness, their pages forever marked by the heat and hunger of the men who dared to bring literature to life.

Morning After Desire

The pale dawn light spilled across their tangled bodies, highlighting the sheen of sweat still clinging to their skin. The office, littered with discarded clothes and open books, bore the evidence of their night—an odyssey of passion and lust woven into the fabric of the room.

Max stirred first, his fingers lazily tracing circles on Daniel's back.

"You know," Max murmured, his voice thick with sleep and satisfaction, **"I think we outdid even Wilde last night."**

Daniel chuckled, his lips brushing against Max's chest. **"I doubt Wilde ever imagined his words could inspire something this filthy."**

Max grinned. **"Then we're giving his legacy a modern twist."**

Daniel shifted, propping himself up on one elbow. His fingers danced over Max's abs, teasing with light touches.

"The beauty wasn't just in the words," Daniel said, his voice soft but laced with heat. **"It was in how we embodied them— how we made those desires come alive."**

Max's eyes darkened as he reached up to cup Daniel's jaw. **"And we did more than just bring them to life,"** he whispered. **"We gave them teeth."**

Daniel leaned down, capturing Max's lips in a kiss that started slow but deepened quickly, reigniting the fire that had simmered between them all night. Max groaned as Daniel's tongue explored his mouth, reigniting his hunger.

"**We're not done,**" Max growled, pushing Daniel onto his back and pinning him down.

"**You never are,**" Daniel teased, spreading his legs invitingly.

Unfinished Business

Max's hands roamed Daniel's body, rediscovering the curves and muscles he had worshipped only hours earlier.

"**We could spend all day like this,**" Max said, sliding down to suck a bruise onto Daniel's inner thigh.

"**And we should,**" Daniel shot back, gasping as Max's tongue flicked over his cock, already stiffening again.

Max gripped Daniel's hips, dragging him to the edge of the desk before swallowing him whole.

"**Fuck, Max,**" Daniel groaned, his head falling back as Max's tongue worked him expertly, alternating between deep, wet sucks and teasing flicks over the head.

Max pulled back, letting Daniel's cock fall free with a wet pop.

"**Turn around,**" Max commanded.

Daniel obeyed, pressing his chest to the desk and arching his ass into the air.

"**God, you're perfect,**" Max said, spreading Daniel's cheeks and spitting onto his hole.

Daniel shivered as Max's tongue teased him, licking and pushing inside until Daniel was panting and begging.

"**Please,**" Daniel gasped. "**I need you to fuck me.**"

Max didn't hesitate. He lined himself up, pressing the head of his cock against Daniel's slick entrance.

"You want this?" Max asked, his voice low and demanding.

"Yes—fuck me," Daniel begged, pushing back against him.

Max drove in slowly, letting Daniel feel every inch stretching him open.

"Jesus, Max," Daniel moaned. **"You're so fucking big."**

Max gripped Daniel's hips and began to thrust, each stroke pushing deeper, harder, until the desk shook beneath them.

"You love this, don't you?" Max growled. **"Being bent over like this—fucked like you're mine."**

"I am yours," Daniel gasped, his voice breaking as Max slammed into him.

Max reached around, stroking Daniel's cock in rhythm with his thrusts.

"Come for me," Max ordered.

Daniel's body tightened, his orgasm hitting hard as he spilled onto the desk. Max followed moments later, burying himself deep as he filled Daniel with his release.

Unwritten Pages

They collapsed together, breathing hard, their bodies slick with sweat and cum.

"I don't think I'll ever get enough of you," Daniel said, his voice shaky but satisfied.

Max kissed the back of his neck. **"Good. Because I'm not letting you go."**

Reflections and Promises

As they dressed, Max's gaze lingered on Daniel, his expression softening.

"**We've started something here,**" Max said. "**Something that feels bigger than either of us.**"

Daniel nodded, his fingers brushing over Max's as he handed him his shirt. "**Then let's keep writing it.**"

Max smiled. "**Imagine us reenacting Achilles and Patroclus— or Romeo and Mercutio.**"

Daniel grinned. "**Or pushing boundaries neither of them could even dream of.**"

They stepped into the morning light, their bodies still tingling from the night before, their minds already scripting the next scene.

"**Last night felt like living poetry,**" Daniel said.

Max squeezed his hand. "**And our next chapter is just beginning.**"

LINGERING QUESTIONS

Max's voice softened. "**You're quiet. What's on your mind?**"

Daniel hesitated before answering. "**I don't know. Last night was incredible, but I can't help thinking there's more to us than just this.**"

Max tilted his head. "**More?**"

"**More than just sex,**" Daniel admitted. "**I don't know what it is yet, but I can feel it.**"

Max reached for Daniel's hand. "**Whatever it is, we'll figure it out—together.**"

Daniel smiled, but uncertainty lingered in his eyes as Max's gaze held his.

They both sensed it—their story was far from finished. It was still being written, a tale of lust, love, and discovery that had only just begun.

Unspoken Tensions

They dressed in silence, the rustle of fabric and the snap of buttons echoing louder than any words either man dared to say. The office, once filled with cries of pleasure and raw passion, seemed colder now, its walls pressing in on them like silent witnesses to something fragile and uncertain.

Daniel's eyes lingered on Max as he straightened his tie, transforming once more into the image of professionalism—the commanding professor who had stolen his breath and body the night before. The contrast between the man who had bent him over the desk and the one who now stood, buttoned up, and composed was almost jarring.

"We should do this again soon," Max said, his tone smooth but lacking the fire it had carried earlier.

Daniel forced a smile, though his stomach twisted in knots. **"Yes. We should."**

The words felt hollow, like a script rehearsed too many times.

Walking Away

Daniel's steps were mechanical as he left the office; his body was sore in all the right places, but his mind was restless. Every memory from the night replayed like a fever dream—Max's hungry lips, the bruising grip of his hands, the heat of his body pressing into Daniel's—but now those images felt almost too perfect, too intense to be real.

Was that all it had been? A perfect illusion?

He wanted to believe it was more than that, that what had passed between them had meant something deeper than lust. But the gnawing doubt remained, an unwelcome companion shadowing his every thought.

THE QUESTION OF DESIRE

Back in his quarters, Daniel paced the room, unable to shake the feeling that there was something he wasn't seeing—something Max was holding back.

"What are you hiding?" Daniel whispered to the empty room, his reflection in the mirror offering no answers.

Max had unraveled him with practiced ease, exposing parts of himself Daniel hadn't even known were buried. But Daniel couldn't ignore the guarded look in Max's eyes, the way he had pulled back just as the night began to feel more than physical.

"You don't let yourself get close, do you?" Daniel muttered, dropping onto his bed.

He stared at the ceiling, his skin still tingling with the memory of Max's touch, and wondered how much of himself he had already given away—and how much more he was willing to risk.

OBSESSION AND DOUBT

The ache between Daniel's legs mirrored the ache in his chest. He wanted Max again—wanted him to pin him down, to take him apart, to murmur filthy promises in his ear. But he also wanted answers.

"What are you so afraid of, Max?" Daniel asked aloud, his voice barely above a whisper.

Was it the scandal? The danger of discovery? Or was Max simply using him, treating him like a brief escape from the rigidity of academia?

Daniel's fingers brushed against his own lips, still swollen from Max's kisses, and he felt his resolve harden.

If Max was hiding something, Daniel would find out what it was.

A Dangerous Resolve

Stripping off his clothes, Daniel lay back on the bed, his hand drifting down to his cock as flashes of the night before filled his mind. Max's voice, rough and commanding. Max's hands are demanding and possessive.

"You're mine," Max had growled, thrusting hard and deep.

Daniel's grip tightened as he stroked himself, letting the memory of Max's dominance push him closer to release.

But as he came, shuddering and gasping for Max's name, the emptiness that followed hit hard.

It wasn't enough. He needed more—he needed to know what Max truly wanted from him.

And he was willing to do whatever it took to find out.

12

WHISPERS THROUGH THE AGES

Forbidden Knowledge

The library reading room lay cloaked in shadow, its hallowed walls steeped in centuries of secrets. Tonight, it was no longer a sanctuary of scholarship but a cathedral of desire. Beneath the towering dome of the Radcliffe Camera, two men prepared to rewrite history—not with ink, but with sweat, lust, and whispered promises.

The scent of aged paper and leather-bound tomes mixed with something primal as the men slipped into a secluded alcove, hidden from prying eyes. Their gazes locked, heavy with intent, their bodies already taut with anticipation.

"No one's watching," the taller man murmured, his voice low and edged with hunger.

"Does it matter if they are?" the other replied, stepping closer, his breath hot against the taller man's ear. **"Let them see."**

UNCOVERING DESIRES

Clothes fell away in hurried motions, revealing hard, sculpted bodies honed by sweat and discipline. The taller man, pale and lean, stood in nothing but tight black boxer briefs that strained against his erection, the fabric already damp with need.

The shorter man, darker and more muscular, bared himself completely. His cock hung thick and heavy between his legs, the veins pulsing as his lover dropped to his knees.

"You've been teasing me all day," the taller man whispered, his voice shaky as he traced the outline of his lover's cock with his tongue.

"And now I'm going to ruin you," the shorter man growled, tangling his fingers in the other's hair.

The taller man wasted no time, his lips parting to take his lover's cock into his mouth. He swallowed him slowly, savoring the stretch as the thick shaft filled his throat.

"Fuck," the shorter man hissed, his hips snapping forward. **"Take it. All of it."**

The taller man obeyed, gagging slightly as his lover drove deeper. Saliva pooled at the corners of his lips, slicking his lover's shaft as he sucked harder, his tongue working in tight circles.

"You're such a good boy," the shorter man said, gripping the back of his lover's head and forcing him down further. **"But don't think I'm letting you off easy."**

He pulled out suddenly, his cock glistening, and turned his lover around, pushing him against the cold stone wall.

"Spread your legs," he commanded, his voice rough with need.

The taller man obeyed, pressing his palms against the wall and arching his back, presenting himself.

"Look at you," the shorter man growled, dragging his fingers down the curve of his lover's ass. **"So desperate to be fucked."**

Without warning, he sank to his knees, spreading his lover's cheeks and diving in with his tongue.

"Oh, God—" the taller man gasped, his knees trembling.

The shorter man licked and teased, pushing his tongue inside and working him open with slow, deliberate strokes.

"You taste fucking perfect," he muttered, his voice muffled by flesh.

But it wasn't enough. He stood, spitting into his hand and stroking his cock as he lined himself up.

"Beg me," he ordered, pressing the head against his lover's hole.

"Please," the taller man moaned, pushing back. **"Fuck me. Fill me. Make me yours."**

THE RITUAL OF RELEASE

The shorter man drove in with one hard thrust, stretching his lover wide and forcing a cry from his lips.

"You're so fucking tight," he groaned, gripping the other's hips as he began to move.

The sound of flesh slapping against flesh filled the alcove, mingling with moans and the rustling of books disturbed by their rhythm.

"You love this," the shorter man growled. **"Being used. Being taken right here where anyone could hear you."**

"Yes!" the taller man gasped, his body trembling as his lover pounded into him.

Sweat dripped down their bodies, the heat between them building as the shorter man reached around, stroking his lover's cock in time with his thrusts.

"Come for me," he demanded. **"Come while I'm buried inside you."**

The taller man's body went rigid, his orgasm hitting hard as he spilled onto the cold stone wall. The tightening of his muscles sent the shorter man over the edge, his growl turning to a low moan as he filled his lover, thrusting until every drop was claimed.

Echoes of Desire

They collapsed together, panting, their bodies slick and trembling.

"We just became part of history," the taller man said, his voice shaky but satisfied.

The shorter man smirked, brushing his lips along his lover's neck. **"We've written our own chapter."**

NEW BEGINNINGS

They dressed slowly, their fingers lingering over each other's skin as if reluctant to let the moment end.

"Next time," the shorter man said, buttoning his shirt, **"we'll find somewhere even riskier."**

The taller man grinned. **"You'll have to try harder than that to scare me."**

As they stepped back into the library's shadows, the walls seemed to hum with secrets, guarding their encounter like so many before. They had become another story woven into its history—a tale of forbidden passion, whispered names, and bodies tangled between knowledge and desire.

. . .

FORBIDDEN PASSION

The library, cloaked in shadows and secrets, bore witness to the forbidden bond between Daniel and Max—a bond forged in whispers, stolen glances, and desperate touches. Graduation loomed, threatening to sever the fragile thread that tied them together. Daniel, poised to begin a new chapter in London, felt the weight of uncertainty pressing against his chest. Meanwhile, Max, the revered professor at St. Anne's College, stood rooted in a life of academic prestige, yet undone by the younger man who had claimed his heart.

"**You know this can't last,**" Max murmured, his voice trembling as he traced the curve of Daniel's jaw.

"**Then let's make every moment count,**" Daniel replied, his fingers slipping beneath Max's shirt, trailing heat along his skin.

Max groaned, surrendering to the inevitability of his desire as Daniel sank to his knees.

Daniel's lips found their mark, enveloping Max's cock in wet, hungry heat. Max braced himself against the heavy desk, his knuckles whitening as Daniel's tongue teased the sensitive head before taking him deeper.

"**God, Daniel,**" Max moaned, threading his fingers through Daniel's hair. "**You're going to make me lose control.**"

Daniel responded with a low hum, the vibration sending shivers through Max's body. He gripped Daniel's head, guiding his movements with slow, deliberate thrusts.

"**Take it,**" Max growled. "**Every inch.**"

Daniel obeyed, swallowing him down until his throat constricted, eliciting a sharp gasp from Max. He reached up, cupping Max's balls and squeezing just enough to make him shudder.

"Don't stop," Max pleaded, his voice breaking as Daniel's tongue worked him closer to the edge.

With a strangled cry, Max came hard, his release spilling down Daniel's throat. Daniel swallowed every drop, savoring the taste as he gazed up at Max with adoration.

Echoes of History

Max leaned down, pulling Daniel to his feet and crushing their lips together in a searing kiss.

"You have no idea what you do to me," Max whispered, his hands roaming Daniel's body.

Daniel smiled, pressing their foreheads together. **"I think I do."**

Their eyes locked, and in that moment, Daniel felt the weight of history pressing down around them. The library, steeped in secrets and scandals, had been a sanctuary for forbidden love for centuries.

"Can you feel it?" Daniel asked. **"The ghosts of all the lovers who came before us—who dared to defy the rules and claim what they wanted?"**

Max nodded, his fingers trailing down Daniel's chest. **"We're part of them now."**

Daniel's hands moved with reverence, mapping the lines of Max's body as if committing him to memory. He pressed kisses along Max's neck, down his chest, and across his stomach, savoring every inch.

"You're mine tonight," Daniel whispered, his voice thick with hunger.

"**Always**," Max replied, surrendering as Daniel pushed him onto the desk.

Daniel wasted no time, spreading Max's legs and diving in, his tongue tracing circles around Max's sensitive rim before pushing inside. Max's moans filled the room, raw and unrestrained.

"**Yes—fuck, Daniel!**" Max cried out, his hips rocking against Daniel's mouth.

Daniel worked him relentlessly, his fingers joining his tongue to stretch him open.

"**You're so fucking perfect,**" Daniel murmured, stroking himself as he prepared to take Max.

"**Do it,**" Max begged. "**I need you inside me.**"

Daniel slicked himself, lining up and pushing inside with one slow, deliberate thrust.

"**Jesus, Max—you're so tight,**" Daniel groaned, gripping Max's hips as he sank deeper.

"**Harder,**" Max demanded. "**Don't hold back.**"

Their rhythm built quickly—needy, primal. The sound of skin slapping against skin echoed off the stone walls, mingling with their gasps and cries.

"**You love being fucked like this, don't you?**" Daniel growled, pounding harder.

"**Yes—fuck—yes!**" Max shouted, his body trembling as Daniel drove him to the brink.

Daniel reached around, stroking Max's cock in time with his thrusts.

"**Come with me,**" Daniel ordered, his voice sharp.

Max obeyed, his release spilling onto the desk as Daniel followed, burying himself deep with a guttural groan.

REFLECTIONS IN THE AFTERGLOW

Their bodies collapsed together, slick with sweat and cum, their hearts pounding in unison. Daniel brushed damp hair from Max's forehead, pressing a lingering kiss to his lips.

"We're part of this place now," Daniel murmured. **"Another story written into its walls."**

Max smiled, his eyes softening. **"And we're just getting started."**

Facing the Future

As they dressed, the weight of reality crept back in. Max adjusted his tie, his movements precise, but Daniel caught the flicker of hesitation in his eyes.

"What happens when I leave?" Daniel asked quietly.

Max paused, then met Daniel's gaze. **"We'll find a way."**

Daniel wanted to believe him. He wanted to trust that this connection—their passion, their love—was strong enough to survive the distance, the doubts, and the secrets.

"I don't want this to end," Daniel admitted.

Max stepped closer, cupping Daniel's face. **"Then it won't. Whatever happens, we're in this together."**

The promise lingered in the air as they stepped into the morning light, their bodies marked by passion and their hearts bound by something deeper than desire.

Their story wasn't over—it was only the beginning.

. . .

Echoes of Desire

The warm glow of the library's lamps cast golden halos across the darkened room, illuminating rows of ancient books and manuscripts. Daniel and Max sat close, their shoulders brushing as they poured over stories of forbidden love—histories written in ink but lived in secret. The scent of leather and parchment mingled with the faint musk of their earlier rendezvous, a reminder of the passion simmering beneath their academic façade.

Daniel traced his fingers over the worn edges of a leather-bound tome, his eyes lingering on a passage that stirred something deep inside him.

"Look at this," he said softly, pointing to a description of two Renaissance lovers who had risked everything to be together. **"Their passion was so intense it transcended time and place."**

Max leaned in, his breath warm against Daniel's neck as he read over his shoulder.

"Incredible," Max murmured, his voice rough and low. **"Their love still speaks to us, even centuries later."**

History Repeating

As the hours slipped by, their hands grazed each other's, their legs pressed together beneath the table, and their whispers grew heavier. The stories they uncovered—of passion, sacrifice, and devotion—felt less like history and more like reflections of their own lives.

"Do you ever feel like we're living out our version of one of these stories?" Daniel asked, his voice barely more than a whisper.

Max looked up, his eyes dark with something unreadable. **"What do you mean?"**

Daniel gestured toward the open books between them. **"Men risking everything for love. That's what these stories are about—and here we are, doing the same thing."**

Max's lips curved into a faint smile as he ran his fingers over the worn cover of the book in front of him.

"You're right," he said. **"Our love is forbidden in some ways, but it's also powerful—and worth every risk."**

Daniel reached out, lacing their fingers together. **"Exactly. We may not face the same dangers, but what we have still matters. It's still something worth fighting for."**

TEMPTATION IN THE STACKS

The tension shifted as Daniel's thumb brushed over Max's knuckles, and the air between them thickened. Max's gaze lingered, his eyes falling to Daniel's lips before flicking back up.

"I can't stop thinking about last night," Max confessed.

"Then don't," Daniel replied, his voice edged with heat. **"We're alone. No one will disturb us."**

Max stood, closing the books and tugging Daniel to his feet.

"You're dangerous," Max said, his lips grazing Daniel's ear.

"And you love it," Daniel shot back, pressing Max against the towering shelves and capturing his mouth in a searing kiss.

CLAIMING THE MOMENT

With a sharp tug, Max's tie came undone, and Daniel shoved his shirt open, the buttons clattering to the floor.

"Fuck, Daniel," Max groaned as Daniel's lips trailed down his neck, biting and sucking until marks bloomed on his skin.

Daniel dropped to his knees, unfastening Max's belt and yanking his trousers down. Max's cock sprang free, thick and hard, and Daniel wasted no time, wrapping his lips around it and taking him deep.

"Jesus—yes," Max hissed, his hands gripping the shelves behind him for support as Daniel's mouth worked him expertly.

Daniel sucked harder, his tongue swirling around the head before plunging down again, his throat tightening as Max thrust into him.

"You love having my cock down your throat, don't you?" Max growled.

Daniel moaned in response, his hands sliding up Max's thighs as he hollowed his cheeks and swallowed him deeper.

Max pulled Daniel to his feet and spun him around, pressing him against the shelf.

"Your turn," Max whispered, pulling down Daniel's jeans and exposing his bare ass.

Max knelt, spreading Daniel open and diving in with his tongue.

"Oh, fuck—Max!" Daniel gasped, his hands bracing against the shelf as Max devoured him, his tongue pushing inside and teasing him until Daniel's legs trembled.

Max stood, slicking himself and pressing the head of his cock against Daniel's hole.

"Beg me," Max ordered.

"**Please,**" Daniel whimpered. "**I need you inside me.**"

Max pushed in slowly, stretching Daniel until he moaned.

"**You feel so fucking good,**" Max groaned, gripping Daniel's hips as he began to move.

Their rhythm built, faster and harder, the sound of skin slapping against skin echoing through the library.

"**You're mine,**" Max growled. "**Say it.**"

"**I'm yours—fuck—always yours,**" Daniel gasped, his body arching as Max drove deeper.

"**Come for me,**" Max commanded, reaching around to stroke Daniel's cock.

Daniel cried out, his orgasm hitting hard as Max followed, spilling inside him with a guttural moan.

A NEW CHAPTER

They collapsed together, their bodies slick with sweat and trembling from release.

"**We just wrote our own story,**" Daniel said, his voice breathless.

Max smirked, brushing his lips along Daniel's neck. "**And I can't wait to write the next chapter.**"

As they dressed, the library seemed to hum with the echoes of their passion—a reminder that their story, like those recorded in the books surrounding them, was timeless and eternal.

13
SEX AND SYMBOLISM

Bound by Words

The dim glow of the library's lamps bathed the shelves in golden light as Daniel and Max lost themselves in the world of books, their fingers brushing against worn spines and weathered pages. Each text seemed to whisper secrets of passion, longing, and defiance—echoes of their own forbidden romance.

Daniel paused, pulling *The Alchemist* from the shelf and flipping through its pages.

"It's about chasing treasure," he murmured. **"But it's really about finding yourself—and risking everything to follow your heart."**

Max leaned in close, his breath warm against Daniel's neck.

"Sound familiar?" Max teased, his voice low.

Daniel smiled but felt the weight of the words settle over him. **"Yeah. It's like us—always searching. Always wanting more."**

Max touched Daniel's arm, his fingers lingering. **"And we'll find it. Together."**

Temptation and Reflection

Another title caught Max's eye—*The Picture of Dorian Gray*. He pulled it from the shelf, his expression darkening as he turned to Daniel.

"You know this one?" Max asked, holding the book out.

Daniel took it, his fingers brushing Max's. **"A man who gives up his soul for beauty—and loses himself in pleasure."**

Max smirked. **"I think you'd get along with Dorian."**

Daniel arched an eyebrow. **"I think you'd want to corrupt him."**

Their eyes locked, and the tension between them sharpened.

"Maybe I already have," Max said, stepping closer.

The conversation dissolved as Daniel grabbed Max's tie and pulled him into a kiss that was anything but scholarly. Their lips collided, tongues battling for dominance as Max pressed Daniel back against the shelves.

"Quiet," Max whispered, biting Daniel's lower lip. **"Unless you want the whole library to hear how badly you need this."**

Daniel moaned, his hands sliding under Max's shirt to tease his nipples.

"Fuck, Max," Daniel growled. **"I can't wait any longer."**

Max's hands were already at Daniel's belt, undoing it with practiced ease before pushing his trousers down.

"**Turn around,**" Max commanded, his voice rough.

Daniel obeyed, bracing himself against the shelves as Max knelt behind him.

DEVOURING DESIRE

Max spread Daniel's cheeks, dragging his tongue over the sensitive skin and teasing his entrance.

"**Jesus, Max—yes!**" Daniel hissed, his knees trembling as Max's tongue pushed inside him.

Max gripped Daniel's hips, pulling him closer as he worked him open, licking and sucking until Daniel was a writhing mess.

"**I need you inside me,**" Daniel begged.

Max stood, unzipping his trousers and stroking himself as he slicked his cock.

"**You're going to take every inch,**" Max growled, pressing the head against Daniel's hole.

"**Do it,**" Daniel demanded. "**Fuck me.**"

Max thrust in slowly, stretching Daniel until he moaned.

"**You're so fucking tight,**" Max groaned, gripping Daniel's hips as he began to move.

"**Harder,**" Daniel ordered, pushing back to meet each thrust. "**I want to feel it.**"

Max complied, slamming into him, the sound of skin on skin filling the library's silence.

"**You love being fucked like this, don't you?**" Max growled.

"Yes—God, yes!" Daniel cried out.

Max reached around, stroking Daniel's cock in time with his thrusts.

"Come for me," Max demanded.

Daniel's body tensed as his orgasm ripped through him, his cum splattering against the shelves. Max followed moments later, burying himself deep and filling Daniel with a guttural groan.

Echoes of the Past

They collapsed against each other, panting, their bodies slick with sweat and cum.

"We just rewrote history," Daniel said breathlessly, looking back over his shoulder.

Max smirked, pressing a kiss to Daniel's neck. **"And we're not finished yet."**

They dressed in silence, the weight of their encounter settling around them like the dust on the old volumes lining the shelves. Max picked up *Giovanni's Room* and opened it to a highlighted passage.

"'Love him and let him love you,'" Max read aloud, his voice soft. **"Do you think we'll ever get to live like that?"**

Daniel stepped closer, taking the book from Max's hands and closing it gently.

"We already are," Daniel replied. **"We're just writing it in secret."**

Max smiled, his hand brushing Daniel's cheek. **"Then let's keep writing."**

The library seemed to hum with the echoes of their passion, adding their story to the countless others hidden in its walls. And as they stepped back into the shadows, their fingers laced together, Daniel knew this was only the beginning.

Bound by Shadows

With practiced ease born from nights of unrestrained passion, Max sank to his knees before Daniel, the weight of desire pressing down on both of them as heavily as the towering bookshelves surrounding them.

In one swift motion, Max freed Daniel's thickening cock from the confines of his trousers and briefs, the sudden exposure making Daniel's breath hitch. The air around them crackled with tension —desperate, electric, and forbidden.

"You've wanted this all night, haven't you?" Max whispered, his voice low and rough.

Daniel groaned, his fingers threading through Max's hair. **"You know I have. Now stop teasing and take it."**

Max smirked before opening his mouth and swallowing Daniel's cock, the warmth and wetness making Daniel's knees nearly buckle.

A Silent Sanctuary

The faint creak of floorboards and distant whispers only heightened the thrill of their hidden encounter. Ancient books lined the walls, bearing silent witness to their carnal acts—keepers of secrets and forbidden knowledge.

Daniel's grip tightened in Max's hair as his lover worked him with lips and tongue, a sinful rhythm that sent waves of pleasure rippling through his body.

"Fuck, Max," Daniel hissed, biting down on his knuckle to keep from crying out.

Max hummed in response, the vibration shooting straight to Daniel's core as Max's tongue swirled around the head of his cock, teasing and coaxing.

The scent of sex mingled with old paper and leather, creating an intoxicating atmosphere that felt timeless—an erotic echo of lovers who had come before them, daring to seize pleasure in the shadows.

Lost in sensation, Daniel felt the pressure building, his muscles tensing as Max's mouth pushed him closer to the edge.

"I'm gonna come," Daniel groaned, his hips bucking forward.

Max didn't pull away. Instead, he took Daniel deeper, his tongue working relentlessly until Daniel's climax crashed over him.

"Max—fuck—yes!" Daniel gasped, spilling into Max's mouth as his body shuddered with release.

Max swallowed every drop, his lips trailing up Daniel's stomach and chest before standing and capturing his mouth in a searing kiss.

"You taste like sin," Max murmured, biting Daniel's lip.

"And you love it," Daniel replied, smirking as he tugged Max's tie, pulling him in for another kiss.

They stood together, breathless and disheveled, their fingers lingering as they helped each other straighten clothes and restore appearances.

"No one will ever know," Max said, his voice steady but his eyes alight with mischief.

"Except these walls," Daniel replied, glancing at the shelves around them. **"They'll keep our secrets."**

They stepped out of the alcove, their bodies still humming with the aftershocks of pleasure, their eyes locked in a silent promise—this wouldn't be the last time.

Rumors and Revelations

But as the days passed, whispers began to ripple through the library—persistent murmurs of stolen glances and late-night disappearances. The tension mounted, as palpable as the scent of dust and ink that filled the air.

Daniel and Max noticed the shift immediately. Fellow students paused mid-conversation as they walked by. Professors exchanged subtle nods, their eyes lingering too long.

The library's sanctuary felt smaller now, its walls closing in as rumors curled through the stacks like smoke.

"Do you think they know?" Daniel asked one evening as they sat together in a secluded corner, their books open but unread.

Max reached for a worn volume of poetry, his fingers brushing Daniel's—a deliberate touch that sent a shiver down Daniel's spine.

"Let them wonder," Max said, his voice low and edged with defiance. **"I'm not hiding this. Not anymore."**

Daniel swallowed hard, his pulse quickening. **"Are you sure? What if—"**

Max cut him off with a kiss, deep and commanding, pulling him closer despite the risk.

"We've already written our names into these walls," Max whispered against Daniel's lips. **"Let them talk. We're not the first, and we won't be the last."**

. . .

A Forbidden Legacy

They returned to their reading, but neither could focus. Daniel's thoughts drifted to the lovers whose stories they'd unearthed in dusty manuscripts—men who had dared to carve out spaces for their desires despite the world's attempts to erase them.

"This place has seen it all," Daniel murmured, flipping through a passage in *Giovanni's Room*. **"And now it sees us."**

Max smirked. **"We're adding another chapter to its history."**

Daniel leaned closer, his lips brushing Max's ear. **"And I can't wait to see what comes next."**

"We're becoming quite the topic of conversation," Max murmured, his gaze locked on Daniel's, a glint of mischief flickering in his eyes.

Daniel's response was a smirk that barely masked the pounding of his heart. **"Let them talk,"** he said, though the adrenaline in his veins betrayed his nonchalance. **"They can't possibly imagine what we share."**

Their eyes lingered for a moment longer before falling reluctantly back to their books. But the words on the pages blurred as memories invaded—the feel of fevered flesh, the scrape of teeth against the skin, and the echo of moans absorbed into the library's ancient walls.

Fueling the Fire

Later, as they wandered through dimly lit aisles flanked by towering shelves, snippets of conversation caught their ears.

"Have you heard about those two?" came a hushed voice from behind a folio. **"They're definitely more than study partners."**

Daniel's heart stuttered, but Max's smirk deepened, a wicked gleam lighting his features.

"Perhaps we should give them more to talk about," Max whispered, his breath hot against Daniel's ear.

The suggestion sent a jolt of heat through Daniel, his pulse quickening at the sheer audacity. He met Max's gaze and nodded, his blood thrumming with the thrill of the risk.

They slipped into the shadows, retreating to a secluded corner where the light dimmed, and the risk of discovery only heightened their hunger.

Max's hands found Daniel first, pulling him close as their mouths met in a kiss that shattered restraint.

"You drive me fucking crazy," Max growled, already working on Daniel's belt.

"Then do something about it," Daniel shot back, his voice thick with need.

Max didn't need more encouragement. He tugged Daniel's belt free, the sound of leather sliding through loops punctuating the charged silence.

Daniel's trousers fell open, and Max's hand slid inside, finding him hard and ready.

"You're already dripping," Max murmured, stroking him through the thin fabric. **"You've been thinking about this all day, haven't you?"**

Daniel groaned, his head falling back as Max knelt, his fingers hooking into Daniel's waistband and dragging his trousers and briefs down in one smooth motion.

Max paused to admire the sight before him—Daniel's cock, thick and flushed, already leaking.

"You're killing me," Daniel hissed, his voice trembling.

Max smirked. **"Not yet. But I'll take care of you."**

And then he did.

Max's mouth closed around Daniel, the sudden heat making Daniel's knees buckle. He braced himself against the bookshelf as Max's tongue worked him with skill and precision, teasing and devouring in equal measure.

"Fuck, Max—just like that," Daniel gasped, his fingers digging into Max's hair, guiding his movements.

Max took him deeper, his throat flexing as he swallowed, pulling back just enough to flick his tongue over the tip before diving down again.

A DANGEROUS RHYTHM

The wet sounds of Max's mouth and Daniel's ragged breathing filled the secluded space, an obscene melody that harmonized with the faint rustle of pages and distant footsteps.

Max's hands roamed, one gripping Daniel's hip while the other cupped his balls, massaging them gently but firmly.

"God, you're good at this," Daniel groaned, his hips jerking forward.

Max hummed in response, the vibration sending shockwaves through Daniel's body.

"Don't stop—don't fucking stop," Daniel begged, his voice barely more than a whisper.

Max's pace quickened, his head bobbing faster as he sensed Daniel's climax building.

"I'm close," Daniel warned, tugging at Max's hair to hold him steady.

Max didn't pull back. Instead, he deepened his strokes, sucking harder until Daniel came with a strangled gasp, spilling down Max's throat.

Max swallowed every drop, his hands still stroking Daniel's thighs as the aftershocks rippled through him.

"Holy fuck," Daniel whispered, his chest heaving.

Max stood, licking his lips as he leaned in for a kiss. **"You taste even better when you're desperate,"** he murmured.

They straightened their clothes with practiced ease, brushing away any evidence of their tryst. But as they stepped out of the shadows, their composure barely masked the fire still simmering beneath the surface.

Two librarians passed them without so much as a glance, yet Daniel couldn't shake the sense that the walls themselves had witnessed everything.

"We got away with it," Daniel muttered, his voice laced with disbelief.

Max grinned, slipping his hand along Daniel's lower back. **"For now."**

Written in Desire

Back at their table, their knees touched beneath the surface. Their connection was as undeniable as the whispered rumors now swirling through the library.

"They're definitely talking about us," Daniel said, his voice low.

"**Let them,**" Max smirked, leaning in close enough for his breath to graze Daniel's ear. "**They're just jealous they can't have what we do.**"

Their fingers brushed over open pages as if daring the words themselves to come alive. With every glance and every secret touch, they etched another line into the story only they could tell —one filled with desire, danger, and defiance.

And as the lamps burned low, casting shadows against the towering shelves, Daniel knew their tale was far from over.

14
SEX TUTORIAL

Confronting Desire

Daniel sat stiffly in the worn leather chair across from Max, his pulse pounding against the tension that filled the office. The walls, lined with books and relics of academia, seemed to press in, amplifying the weight of their secret. The air was thick, charged with a mixture of longing, frustration, and unspoken fears.

"Max," Daniel said, his voice strained but resolute. **"We can't keep living like this."**

Max's gaze flitted nervously to the window before landing on Daniel. The vulnerability in his eyes was raw, edged with longing and regret.

"I know," Max whispered, his voice barely audible. **"But what can we do? Our relationship is forbidden. I don't want to lose you."**

Daniel leaned forward, bridging the physical space between them, and took Max's hand. His grip was firm, reassuring.

"**We can't let fear control us,**" Daniel said. "**We have to fight for this—for us.**"

Max's fingers tightened around Daniel's, his expression shifting from doubt to determination.

"**You're right,**" Max said, his voice steadying. "**But how do we face a world determined to keep us apart?**"

Daniel's eyes burned with conviction. "**Together. We face it together.**"

Max's lips parted, his breath quickening. "**I want that,**" he said softly. "**I want you—no matter what it takes.**"

Breaking the Chains

The heat between them flared. Words gave way to action as Daniel surged forward, claiming Max's lips in a fierce and unapologetic kiss. Their tongues met, sliding together with a hunger that left them gasping.

"**We don't hide anymore,**" Daniel said between breaths.

Max pulled him closer, his voice thick with need. "**Show me.**"

Daniel stepped back, his hands trembling slightly as he reached into Max's desk drawer. He withdrew a pair of black underwear—tight, sleek, and teasingly scandalous. Tossing them onto the desk, he locked eyes with Max.

"**Take these,**" Daniel said, his voice low but commanding. "**Let's show them how far we're willing to go.**"

Max's gaze dropped to the underwear, understanding flickering in his eyes. He stood, pulling his shirt over his head and tossing it aside, his toned chest exposed.

"No more hiding," Max said, his voice rough as he peeled away his trousers, leaving him in nothing but the snug black briefs that hugged his arousal.

Daniel mirrored him, stripping down until they stood before each other—bare, vulnerable, and ready.

Max closed the distance, his hands roaming over Daniel's chest, tracing the hard lines of muscle and pausing to tweak his nipples.

"You're fucking perfect," Max murmured, his breath hot against Daniel's neck.

Daniel tilted his head back, surrendering to the sensation as Max kissed and nipped along his jawline.

"I want you," Max said, his voice hoarse with need. **"Right here. Right now."**

"Then take me," Daniel replied, his words dripping with urgency.

Max shoved him back against the desk, knocking papers and books aside as he claimed Daniel's mouth again. Their bodies collided, skin against skin, as Max's hands dropped to unfasten Daniel's briefs.

The fabric hit the floor, and Max fell to his knees, gripping Daniel's cock and taking it into his mouth without hesitation.

Consuming Heat

Daniel gasped, his hands tangling in Max's hair as his lover's tongue teased and swirled, working him to full hardness.

"Fuck, Max," Daniel groaned. **"You're going to make me come already."**

Max pulled back just enough to smirk. **"Not yet. I'm not done with you."**

Standing, Max spun Daniel around and bent him over the desk, spreading him wide.

"Stay still," Max ordered, grabbing the lube from the drawer and slicking his fingers.

Daniel shivered as Max's fingers worked him open, stretching and teasing until Daniel was begging.

"Please, Max—fuck me," Daniel pleaded, pressing back against his hand.

Max didn't make him wait. He slicked himself and pressed the head of his cock against Daniel's hole, pushing in slowly, inch by inch.

"God, you feel so good," Max growled, gripping Daniel's hips as he began to thrust.

"Harder," Daniel demanded. **"Don't hold back."**

Max obeyed, pounding into him with relentless force, their bodies slapping together as the desk creaked beneath them.

"You love this," Max said through gritted teeth. **"Being bent over my desk like this—fucked where anyone could find us."**

"Yes—fuck, yes!" Daniel cried, his fingers clutching the edge of the desk as Max drove him closer to the edge.

Max reached around, gripping Daniel's cock and stroking him in time with his thrusts.

"Come for me," Max commanded. **"Now."**

Daniel's body tensed, his orgasm ripping through him as he spilled onto the desk. Max followed moments later, groaning as he filled Daniel with his release.

. . .

AFTER THE FALL

They collapsed together, their breaths ragged, their bodies slick with sweat. Max pressed a lingering kiss to the back of Daniel's neck.

"We're not hiding anymore," Max said softly.

Daniel turned, his eyes blazing. **"No. We're not."**

They dressed in silence, exchanging heated glances as they smoothed their clothes. When they finally stepped out of the office, the world seemed to hum with possibility—both thrilling and dangerous.

As they walked side by side, their hands brushed—an electric current passing between them.

Their story was no longer confined to whispers. It had become an act of defiance, a testament to love that refused to be hidden.

Daniel's arms encircled Max; their bodies pressed so tightly together that it felt impossible to tell where one ended, and the other began. Sweat slicked their skin, heightening the friction as they moved in a primal rhythm—raw and relentless.

"God, Daniel—don't stop," Max gasped, his voice ragged with need.

"I'm not stopping until I've had every inch of you," Daniel growled, biting down on Max's shoulder before capturing his lips in a bruising kiss.

Their tongues tangled, a clash of hunger and desperation as they teetered on the edge of release. The scent of leather, old paper, and sex filled the air, mingling into something forbidden and intoxicating.

"Come with me," Max pleaded, his hands clutching Daniel's back like he was afraid to let go.

Daniel thrust harder, their bodies locked in a dance that promised to shatter them both.

"Together," Daniel growled, biting down on Max's neck as pleasure exploded through them, their cries muffled against each other's skin.

Afterglow and Gratitude

They collapsed in a tangle of limbs, their hearts pounding in sync as the aftershocks of their release slowly ebbed. Max's head rested on Daniel's chest, his breath warm against his skin.

"Thank you," Max whispered, his voice trembling. **"Thank you for giving me this—for showing me what love feels like."**

Daniel's hand traced lazy patterns down Max's spine, his own heart swelling. **"You don't have to thank me,"** he murmured. **"You've given me just as much."**

Max shifted, propping himself up on one elbow to meet Daniel's gaze. The flicker of vulnerability in his eyes sent a pang of protectiveness through Daniel.

"I was afraid," Max admitted. **"Afraid that wanting this—wanting you—would cost me everything."**

Daniel cupped his face. **"We're not going to lose this."**

Unveiling Truths

Later, surrounded by the library's hushed reverence, Daniel and Max sat in the shadowed recesses of the stacks, their bodies still humming with the remnants of their passion.

"I never thought I'd find this," Daniel said softly, his fingers brushing over Max's knuckles.

Max tilted his head, studying him. **"Find what?"**

"Someone who sees me—the real me—and doesn't run."

Max's grip tightened. **"I'm not running, Daniel. I won't."**

They sat there, the weight of their confession settling between them like another secret to keep—but this one felt less like a burden and more like an anchor.

"It's not just about us," Daniel said suddenly. **"It's about standing up to all of it—the whispers, the judgment, the rules meant to keep us apart."**

Max leaned back, running his hand over an open book, its pages filled with ancient stories of forbidden love. **"We're not the first,"** he said. **"And we won't be the last."**

Daniel's voice sharpened. **"But we're here now, and we're not hiding anymore."**

Max's eyes burned with a new determination as he nodded. **"Then let's write our own story—one no one can erase."**

Carving Their Legacy

Daniel led Max deeper into the library, their footsteps echoing softly against the stone floors. The glow of an overhead lamp cast their shadows long against the shelves as Daniel stopped before a glass case containing an ancient manuscript.

"This is where we make history," Daniel said, gesturing to the text bathed in golden light.

Max stepped closer, his fingers brushing the glass. **"Read it to me,"** he whispered.

Daniel opened the case, carefully turning the fragile pages until he found the passage he sought.

"And so they stood, side by side, against the tide of uncertainty, their love the compass that guided them through the storm."

Max swallowed hard. **"That's us."**

Daniel turned to him, his eyes blazing. **"Then let's make sure our storm doesn't tear us apart."**

Max reached for Daniel, pulling him close as their lips met again, this time slower but no less intense.

"We'll keep fighting," Max murmured against his mouth. **"For this. For us."**

Daniel smiled, his fingers curling into Max's shirt. **"We're already winning."**

They lingered in the glow of the manuscript; their bodies flush with heat as they silently vowed to protect what they'd built—no matter what it cost them.

The library, their sanctuary of knowledge and desire, bore silent witness as they pressed forward, leaving another chapter of their story etched into its shadows.

Epic and Enduring

Daniel's fingertips trailed along the sharp edge of Max's jaw, his touch soft but charged with intent. Their eyes locked, and in that moment, the air between them pulsed with unspoken promises.

"We'll be like those tales," Daniel said, his voice low but certain. **"Epic and enduring."**

Max's lips curved into a smile—a knowing, secretive thing that sent heat straight through Daniel's core.

"You really believe that?" Max asked.

"I do," Daniel replied, his tone unwavering. **"We'll write our own legend, one they'll never forget."**

They stood in the dim glow of the library, their connection vibrating with the weight of history and desire. Their fingers intertwined, not just a gesture of affection but an act of defiance —a refusal to be erased or hidden.

ESCAPING SHADOWS

As they left the exhibit and returned to the library's main hall, the murmur of voices and the shuffle of feet reminded them that the outside world awaited—judgmental, prying, and unrelenting.

Daniel squeezed Max's hand, unwilling to let go even as they neared the exit.

"Do you think we'll ever be free of all this secrecy?" Daniel asked, his voice tinged with vulnerability.

Max's gaze softened, though his answer was edged with reality. **"Maybe not completely,"** he admitted. **"But we have moments like these—our own quiet rebellion."**

Daniel leaned in, brushing his lips softly against Max's—a lingering, deliberate kiss right there in the library's shadowed archway.

"Then let's make every moment count," Daniel whispered, his breath hot against Max's mouth.

Max's eyes darkened. **"Let's."**

. . .

CLAIMING THE NIGHT

The cool night air wrapped around them as they stepped outside. The cobbled streets of Oxford stretched ahead, and their steps echoed softly as they passed centuries-old buildings and shuttered shops.

The weight of history surrounded them, yet the night belonged solely to them—a bubble of freedom amidst the constraints of academia and expectation.

They didn't speak much as they wandered through alleys and courtyards, their hands brushing occasionally before clasping firmly. Words felt unnecessary when each look, each shared glance, said everything.

Eventually, they arrived at Max's flat—a small, cluttered space bursting with books, artifacts, and half-finished manuscripts. It was as if the past had taken root here, spilling across every surface in organized chaos.

Daniel ran his fingers over the cool glass of a display case, admiring the delicate details of a Roman coin set against velvet.

"We could get lost in time here," Daniel mused, his voice reverent as he absorbed the weight of history surrounding them.

Max came up behind him, his body pressing just close enough to make Daniel's pulse quicken. **"And yet,"** Max said, his voice a low murmur, **"I find myself completely present when I'm with you."**

Daniel turned to face him, his lips parting as Max's eyes roamed his face. The silence that followed wasn't empty; it buzzed with possibility, with the heat of things left unsaid.

Max reached out, undoing the first button of Daniel's shirt, his fingers brushing the bare skin beneath.

"**Take this off,**" Max ordered, his voice rough.

Daniel obeyed, shedding his shirt and letting it fall to the floor. Max's eyes darkened as he took in the sight—Daniel's toned chest, the faint marks still visible from their last encounter.

"**You're beautiful,**" Max said, stepping closer and running his hands down Daniel's sides before sliding them around to cup his ass.

Daniel smirked. "**Stop staring and do something about it.**"

Max responded with a growl, capturing Daniel's lips in a hungry kiss as he backed him up against the desk.

Consuming Passion

Max's hands were everywhere—tearing at Daniel's belt, pushing down his trousers until they pooled at his ankles. Daniel's cock sprang free, already hard and aching.

"**You've been wanting this all night, haven't you?**" Max teased, dropping to his knees.

"**Shut up and suck me,**" Daniel demanded, gripping Max's hair and pulling him closer.

Max didn't hesitate, swallowing Daniel's cock deep into his throat. The heat, the pressure, and the obscene wet sounds drove Daniel wild.

"**Fuck, Max,**" Daniel moaned, his hips thrusting forward as Max took him deeper.

Max's hands gripped Daniel's thighs, holding him in place as he worked his tongue, teasing and tasting. Daniel's breaths turned ragged, his moans echoing off the walls as he felt himself losing control.

"I'm close," Daniel warned, but Max didn't pull back.

Instead, he doubled down, his pace quickening until Daniel's orgasm hit—hot, intense, and overwhelming.

Max stood and kissed him, letting Daniel taste himself on his lips.

"You're not done yet," Max whispered, spinning Daniel around and bending him over the desk.

Daniel gasped as Max pressed against him, slick and ready.

"Tell me you want this," Max demanded.

"I want it—I need it," Daniel groaned. **"Fuck me."**

Max didn't hold back. He pushed in, stretching Daniel inch by inch until he was fully seated.

"You feel so fucking good," Max growled, thrusting hard and fast.

Daniel clutched the edges of the desk, his body arching to meet each thrust.

"Harder," Daniel begged. **"Don't stop."**

Max's hand reached around, stroking Daniel's cock in time with his thrusts.

"Come for me again," Max ordered.

Daniel cried out, his body trembling as he came for the second time, his release splattering the desk. Max followed seconds later, groaning as he filled Daniel completely.

EPILOGUE OF DESIRE

Their bodies sagged against each other as the intensity faded, leaving only the steady rhythm of their breaths.

Max pressed a lingering kiss to Daniel's shoulder. **"We'll keep making history,"** he murmured.

Daniel smiled, his fingers curling around Max's hand. **"And no one can erase it."**

In the quiet sanctuary of Max's flat, surrounded by relics of the past, they laid the foundation for a future they refused to hide—a story carved not in stone but in flesh and passion.

Daniel sat rigid in the leather chair across from Max, his pulse racing as he took in the sight of the man who had become both his greatest desire and his greatest risk. The office—normally a sanctuary of intellect and order—felt claustrophobic, heavy with tension and unspoken fears.

"Max," Daniel said softly, his voice trembling. **"We can't keep living like this."**

Max's eyes finally lifted, filled with longing and regret. **"I know,"** he replied, barely above a whisper. **"But what can we do? Our relationship is forbidden. I don't want to lose you."**

Daniel reached across the desk and took Max's hand, threading their fingers together as if anchoring them both.

"We can't let fear control us," Daniel said firmly. **"We have to stand up for ourselves—for this."**

Max exhaled shakily, his expression shifting to one of resolve. **"You're right,"** he said. **"But how do we face a world determined to keep us apart?"**

Daniel leaned in closer, his voice low but charged. **"We face it together. We show them our love is stronger than their rules."**

Max smiled then—a flicker of hope lighting his eyes. **"I want that,"** he said. **"I want us. No matter what it takes."**

. . .

SHATTERING RESTRAINT

Their words dissolved into action. Max stood first, yanking Daniel into a kiss that was anything but restrained. Their mouths collided, tongues tangling in a desperate exchange as years of fear and secrecy melted away.

"I need you," Max murmured between kisses, his breath ragged.

"Then take me," Daniel replied, his voice thick with want. **"Show me we're done hiding."**

Daniel pulled back just long enough to stalk to Max's desk, yanking open a drawer and revealing the contents—candles, lubricant, and two pairs of matching black underwear. He tossed the items onto the desk, his gaze daring Max to follow his lead.

"Put these on," Daniel said, stripping off his own clothes with deliberate slowness.

Max didn't hesitate. He mirrored Daniel's movements, shoving his trousers and underwear down and stepping out of them, revealing his toned, muscular body and the erection straining against the tight black fabric.

"We're doing this," Max said, his voice edged with both defiance and arousal.

Daniel stepped closer, trailing his fingers over Max's chest, teasing his nipples before gripping his hips and pulling him in. Their mouths met again, this time slower but no less intense.

"God, I can't get enough of you," Max groaned, sliding his hands down Daniel's back and cupping his ass.

"Then don't," Daniel challenged, nipping at Max's neck before pushing him back against the desk.

Max groaned as Daniel dropped to his knees, his hands smoothing over Max's thighs before tugging down the underwear. Max's cock sprang free, thick and hard, and Daniel wasted no time wrapping his lips around it.

"Fuck, Daniel," Max hissed, threading his fingers through Daniel's hair and holding him in place as Daniel's mouth worked him with skilled determination.

The wet sounds of suction filled the office as Daniel took him deeper, hollowing his cheeks and moaning around the length.

"You're so fucking good at this," Max groaned, thrusting gently into Daniel's mouth.

Daniel pulled back, his lips slick and swollen.

"I'm not done with you yet," he said, pushing Max onto the desk.

Max spread his legs, exposing himself completely as Daniel reached for the lube.

"You ready for me?" Daniel asked, coating his fingers and pressing one against Max's tight entrance.

"Do it," Max demanded, his voice breaking.

Daniel worked him open, adding another finger, then a third, stretching him until Max was writhing against the desk.

"Fuck me already," Max growled, his hands gripping the edge of the desk.

Daniel slicked his cock and lined himself up, teasing Max's hole before pressing in slowly.

"You feel so good," Daniel groaned, sinking deeper with every thrust.

"Harder," Max begged, pushing back to meet Daniel's rhythm.

The desk creaked beneath them as their bodies collided, the sharp slap of skin echoing in the confined space.

"You like being fucked like this?" Daniel growled, gripping Max's hips tightly.

"Yes—don't stop!" Max cried out, his body arching as Daniel drove into him with unrelenting force.

Unleashing the Storm

Max reached for his cock, stroking himself furiously as Daniel pounded into him.

"I'm gonna come," Max moaned, his voice breaking.

"Do it—come for me," Daniel ordered, thrusting harder as Max's body tensed.

Max shouted as he climaxed, spurting across the desk in thick streams. The sight pushed Daniel over the edge, and with one final thrust, he came deep inside Max, his body trembling as waves of pleasure rolled through him.

They collapsed together, panting and slick with sweat.

"We're not hiding anymore," Max said breathlessly.

Daniel smiled, brushing a kiss against his lips. **"No. We're not."**

They dressed slowly, stealing glances and touches as if afraid the moment might slip away. When they finally stepped out into the night, their hands found each other's, lacing together in a silent vow.

"Let them talk," Daniel said, his voice steady.

"Let them watch," Max added, his smile wicked.

The streetlights flickered above them, casting long shadows as they walked through Oxford's storied corridors—a new kind of history etched in every step they took.

Stripping Away Fear

Their eyes locked—an unspoken promise exchanged in the heat of shared desire and defiance. Without hesitation, they stripped off their shirts, revealing taut muscles and smooth skin, each body a mirror of strength and vulnerability. The dim glow of the desk lamp cast shadows across their forms, highlighting the contours of their desire.

Daniel stepped closer, his hands steady as he unbuttoned Max's trousers, letting his knuckles brush against Max's erection straining beneath the fabric.

"They want us to be ashamed," Daniel murmured, his lips brushing the sensitive skin of Max's neck before pressing a deliberate kiss to the thrum of his pulse.

Max groaned, his breath ragged as Daniel's hands slipped inside his underwear, gripping him firmly.

"Let them try," Max growled, his voice thick with need.

Their matching black underwear, clinging to their arousals, became more than fabric. It was armor. It was defiance. It was a banner they carried into this war—a refusal to let shame define them.

Max's fingers hooked into the waistband of Daniel's briefs, yanking them down in one swift motion.

"We're more than this secret," Max said, his voice steadier now, charged with conviction.

Daniel stepped out of the discarded material and pressed his bare body against Max's.

"We're a commitment made of flesh," he whispered, his breath warm against Max's lips.

The Heat of Defiance

Their mouths collided—urgent, desperate, unrelenting. The kiss burned, consuming them in flames that neither shame nor judgment could extinguish.

Daniel's hands roamed Max's body, memorizing every ridge, curve, and scar. Max responded in kind, his touch possessive, as though he could anchor Daniel to him through sheer force of will.

"We stand together," Daniel breathed between kisses, his lips swollen and slick.

Max pulled Daniel closer, their erections brushing together and sending shocks of pleasure through both of them.

"Against all odds," Max replied, his voice thick with determination.

The kiss deepened, tongues tangling in a dance as old as time—a push and pull, a declaration of unity that needed no words.

Max shoved Daniel back against the desk, sending papers fluttering to the floor.

"I'm done hiding," Max growled, pressing his weight against Daniel and grinding into him.

Daniel gasped, arching against Max. **"Then show me."**

Max dropped to his knees, his hands sliding down Daniel's hips as he took him into his mouth in one swift, wet motion. Daniel cried out, his fingers threading through Max's hair, guiding him with firm pressure.

"Fuck, Max," Daniel moaned, his voice echoing in the dimly lit office.

Max hummed around him, the vibrations sending jolts of pleasure up Daniel's spine.

"You love this, don't you?" Daniel growled, tightening his grip on Max's hair.

Max pulled off just long enough to smirk. **"I love making you lose control."**

Daniel's head fell back as Max sucked him deeper, his tongue teasing the sensitive tip before taking him all the way down.

"You're going to make me—" Daniel gasped, but Max didn't stop. He doubled his efforts, hollowing his cheeks as Daniel came with a cry, spilling hot and thick down Max's throat.

Max swallowed every drop before standing and kissing Daniel fiercely, letting him taste himself on Max's lips.

Unleashing Desire

Daniel shoved Max back, flipping their positions and pushing him down onto the desk.

"Now it's my turn," Daniel said, his voice dripping with hunger.

Max grinned, spreading his legs as Daniel yanked his underwear down and gripped his cock, stroking it slowly.

"Don't tease me," Max growled.

Daniel smirked. **"I thought you liked it when I took my time."**

But Max was done waiting. **"Fuck me,"** he demanded.

Daniel grabbed the lube from the drawer, slicking his fingers before pressing one inside Max, watching as his lover writhed beneath him.

"You're so tight," Daniel whispered, adding a second finger and curling them just right.

"Stop teasing and fuck me," Max snapped, his voice raw.

Daniel slicked himself and lined up, pushing in slowly.

"God, yes," Max moaned as Daniel filled him inch by inch.

Daniel set a punishing rhythm, pounding into Max and gripping his hips hard enough to leave bruises.

"You like being fucked like this?" Daniel growled.

"Yes—don't stop!" Max cried, his voice breaking.

RISING TO CLIMAX

Max's hand shot down, stroking himself in time with Daniel's thrusts.

"I'm close," Max panted.

Daniel leaned down, biting Max's shoulder. **"Come for me."**

Max shouted as he climaxed, spilling onto his stomach. The sight sent Daniel over the edge, and he followed moments later, filling Max with a guttural groan.

Their bodies sagged against each other, their breaths mingling in the aftermath of their release.

Max turned his head, pressing a kiss to Daniel's jaw. **"We're not just a secret,"** he said softly. **"We're a revolution."**

Daniel brushed his lips against Max's ear. **"And no one can stop us."**

They cleaned up slowly, brushing their fingers as they redressed. Papers lay scattered around the office, a chaotic testament to the passion that had unfolded there.

Max grinned as he tucked his shirt back in. **"I think we just rewrote history."**

Daniel smirked, straightening his tie. **"And we're just getting started."**

Hand in hand, they stepped into the night, their love no longer confined to shadows.

ABOUT THE AUTHOR

Griff Holland—The Master of Sweat, Sin, and Seduction

Griff Holland isn't just an author—he's a force of nature. By day, he's a celebrated architect restoring New England's most treasured historic buildings, leaving his mark one exquisite detail at a time. But by night, Griff trades blueprints for dirty fantasies, crafting raw, unapologetic male erotica that pulses with passion, lust, and desire.

Before setting the literary world on fire, Griff dominated the slopes as a former Olympic skier—a man who knows exactly what it takes to go hard, push limits, and leave it all on the line. He channels that same intensity into every word he writes, delivering stories packed with muscled studs, kinky encounters, and breathtaking tension that keeps readers begging for more.

But Griff's talents don't stop there. He's also a sought-after public speaker and a familiar face on television home repair shows, captivating audiences with his easy charm, rugged good looks, and hands-on expertise. Whether he's restoring a crumbling mansion or stripping his characters bare, Griff's signature style is equal parts polished and provocative.

A lifelong dog lover and outdoor enthusiast, Griff fuels his imagination while hiking trails and conquering mountains with his four-legged companions. And if that weren't enough, his early years as a high school and collegiate football player provide the inspiration for the sweaty locker rooms, jockstrap fantasies, and alpha-male dynamics that pulse through his stories.

Despite his many accomplishments, Griff remains grounded—and insatiable—always chasing the next thrill, the next story, and the next erotic masterpiece. Whether he's carving through fresh powder on the slopes, sweating it out in a gym, or diving into a sizzling sex scene at his desk, Griff does it all with fearless intensity and a fierce commitment to pleasure.

Griff Holland doesn't just write erotic fiction—he lives it.

ACKNOWLEDGMENTS

First and foremost, a massive thank you to the unapologetic lovers of gay erotica—the bold, the kinky, and the downright insatiable readers who keep stories like this alive and throbbing. This collection is for you. The men in my world have found strength in their sensuality—and their sexuality—whether they're hanging out in underwear stores flaunting bulges in designer jockstraps, strutting their stuff in public for all to admire, or secretly pumping out a load of cum into their briefs while we're all watching (and loving it). To all you kinksters, voyeurs, and exhibitionists—you're the real MVPs. Your hunger for stories like this fuels every filthy scene. **You are my heroes.**

To my partner, Mitchell—my rock-hard support system and my go-to wide receiver both on and off the field—you're the man who makes every day sexier. There's nothing quite like coming home to see you sprawled out in sheer micro bikinis or teasing me with a pair of soiled boxer briefs. You've been there to throw me a clean pair of underwear every morning—and sometimes, to rip them off when the moment demanded it. Thank you for always helping me look (and feel) my best, in the locker room and out. I couldn't have done this without you.

To my editor and beta readers—thank you for taking this dirty, messy fantasy and turning it into a polished, panty-soaking reality. Your insights, sharp critiques, and fearless honesty shaped this book into what it is today. You caught every dangling modifier—and let's be real, a few dangling dicks too. I appreciate your dedication to detail and excellence more than words (or moans) can say.

To the LGBTQ+ community—thank you for fighting tirelessly for equality, visibility, and freedom. Your passion and perseverance have created a world where stories like this can be told, shared, and celebrated without shame. Your advocacy makes this space safe for love, lust, and liberation, and your courage is the beating heart behind every word I write.

And finally, to my readers—you glorious, thirsty souls who can't get enough muscle, sweat, and sin. Thank you for diving headfirst into this world with me, for embracing every sultry detail and every forbidden fantasy. Whether this story left you blushing, breathless, or hard as hell, I'm honored you came along for the ride (in every sense of the word). I hope this book brought you pleasure, excitement, and maybe even a new kink or two to explore.

Here's to pushing boundaries, breaking rules, and stripping down to the rawest, realest versions of ourselves. Thank you for making this journey unforgettable.

With love, lust, and a Speedo too tight to breathe in,

Griff

READERS—GOT IDEAS?

Griff Holland Wants Your Dirtiest, Kinkiest Ideas—No Fantasy Too Wild!

Griff Holland—bestselling erotica author and master of steamy, pulse-pounding tales—has hit a tantalizing crossroads. After churning out a relentless stream of erotic hits fueled by sweat, lust, and forbidden desires, Griff's muse is catching its breath. But his fans? They're just getting started.

Earlier this morning, Griff opened his inbox to find it flooded with ideas from his devoted readers—ideas dripping with passion, scandal, and more than a little filth. Some emails painted vivid portraits of muscled studs caught in compromising positions, while others teased barely-there scenarios—a flicker of a glance, a forbidden touch—that begged to be explored.

Griff was humbled—and turned on—by the sheer creativity and kink his readers poured into their suggestions. He knew he had to honor their trust by taking these fantasies to the next level. After all, Griff's superpower is spinning even the most outrageous ideas into fully fleshed-out, toe-curling, underwear-soaking stories. And let's face it—his readers expect nothing less.

So now, Griff is throwing open the floodgates and daring his fans to push the limits even further. Think your idea might be *too much*? Think again. Griff's motto is simple: **"No kink is too kinky."** From locker-room gangbangs to rooftop sex parties, from forbidden coaches to submissive swimmers begging for release—Griff wants it all.

Have a fantasy that's been simmering in your mind? A scene that keeps you up at night? Send it to Griff, and you just might see your idea come to life in his next scandalous, sweat-soaked bestseller.

Email Griff at **Griff.Holland.Writer@gmail.com** and don't hold back. He's waiting—breathless and hard—for your dirtiest, wildest dreams.

Printed in Great Britain
by Amazon

58428971R10116